RETURN TO

THE

OLD

HENDERSON

MINE

Jana Nolan

RETURN TO THE OLD HENDERSON MINE

Jana Nolan

Earth Star Publications
Eckert, Colorado

FIRST EDITION
First Printing October 2018

ISBN 978-0-944851-55-5

Printed in the United States of America

CONTENTS

INTRODUCTION

For those of you that aren't familiar with any of my books, or my style of writing, I would like to say that this one took me on a journey in my mind to bring you stories that will thrill and chill you.

I grew up in a small town called Montrose, Colorado. Being a country girl, many of my stories revolve around country living or a small town atmosphere.

The title, "Return to THE OLD HENDERSON MINE," was chosen by me because of a remake that I wanted to write to take you back in time to a story that was written many years ago. I added on for your enjoyment of this book.

Sit back and get ready for a story that will give your thoughts a ride of a lifetime. After reading my novel, remember that this book is only fiction, or is it?

I will be taking you in two different directions. In the beginning, you will read about an older woman who will tell her story of what she and her husband encountered in a small town in Ireland. She then goes on to tell about what her parents found in a small town called Henderson, Colorado. With a unique gift that she inherited from her mother and grandmother, she explains how all three of them saved the lives of many people through mental telepathy, or better known as "Mind Power."

As with all of my books, I try to give my readers a sense of what could happen to them on any day. Fact or fiction?

Now that I have shared with you a brief summary of what this book is about, it is up to you, the reader, to decide if this tale is capable of happening, or if it is just something that an author such as myself completely made up to captivate her readers.

However you interpret this book, remember that there are strange happenings every day that surround us, or that we find ourselves in the middle of because of bad choices. With all of this in mind, let yourself wander back in time to a different place and time period that will make you think.

Jana Nolan

1

SADNESS AND
WORDS SPOKEN

Today is the day scheduled for my granddaughter and me to make a long trip from Ireland to Colorado, where we will visit an old mine in a small town called Henderson.

Several years ago, my mother and father went there on an assignment from the *Ridgewood Times* newspaper. At that time there were many occurrences happening there that the owner of the newspaper wanted to investigate. He wanted an article to be written by them as this would be big news for a small town.

My name is Amy Peterson Allen. I grew up in California. There I went to a university, where I became a doctor. As I sit at my kitchen table, looking out the window, I am remembering my life and what brought me here.

Many years ago, when the funeral car passed through the cemetery, I turned my head in disbelief toward the window. I had chosen to look one last time at the grave site surrounded by fresh bouquets of flowers.

That day my eyes were filled with tears of sorrow and grief. The person who was lying still and silent in the ground in her coffin was very dear to me. She was my grandmother.

I felt like a big part of my world had been taken from me too soon. Her wisdom, smile and cheerful laugh I would miss deeply.

A few weeks before that day, while I was visiting a town in Ireland, I was offered a job at one of the hospitals here as I had been a doctor in L.A. for several years and was having doubts at that time on whether I should leave my home to move to a new place and country.

I was the youngest born to my mother and father. My sister, Karen, was always the one in school to excel in everyday activities ... and life itself. Her genetics are similar to those of our father. She has blonde hair, blue eyes and a beautiful smile. In her senior year she was voted prom queen, cheerleader, and the most popular girl in her class. I, on the other hand, was the one stuck in the lab, working on a project for biology. After high school, Karen married a man she had met at the university that she attended. He came from a rich family that had made their money from selling textiles.

My older brother, Mark, is also a successful business man. He never got married, and likes being single. He is a quiet man who doesn't talk much. When our mother and father retired from the *Ridgewood Times* newspaper, they decided to buy the company. My father asked Mark to take over as executive manager and he accepted.

That day of my grandmother's funeral, we drove slowly through the cemetery. At that time I was re-minded of a time from my past. My friends and I would spend countless hours playing and hiding behind different tombstones of those people who were lying motionless in the ground throughout eternity. When nighttime came, there were shadows from the trees that would scare my friends. Most of the time they would leave. None of them understood how I could stay in there all alone.

My words to them were, "Why be afraid ... as we all know that eventually we will end up here."

The thought of death never scared me. I believe that no one really dies and that each person lying motionless in the cemetery cannot only see me, but will also keep me company while I am there with them. I was sure that some of my friends thought of me as being strange and unusual. Everyone knows that a good news reporter has to have a good imagination. Otherwise, where in the world would they get some of those strange stories that they write about? My family were newspaper people and so I did come from good and intelligent people.

With me feeling empty inside, I wasn't ready to say goodbye. I knew that she couldn't stay alive forever, and it would take time for me to adjust to her being gone.

The day before my grandmother passed away, I went over to speak to her about Ireland. I had decided to leave LA and move there. I had awakened early that morning and, for some reason, I was having doubts about my decision to leave. After much thought about it, I left my condo and drove up to Santa Barbara to talk to her about it.

When I climbed out of my car and walked up her sidewalk to the front door, I could smell cookies baking in her oven.

We went into her kitchen, where I sat and watched her make chocolate chip and peanut butter cookies. As we talked occasionally, I would take a piece of dough and put it in my mouth.

Grandmother would softly tap my hand and say, "Amy, you are a doctor! You know that eating raw dough isn't good for you." She was right ... I did know better.

As the cookies baked she sat down beside me to

talk. "Amy, there is something that I need to talk to you about. I'm an old woman that's not too sure how much longer she has to spend with you. I've had a good life. Plus I yearn to be with your grandfather again. As you know, you are the image of your mother. There has always been something special about you. We both know what it is that I am referring to."

At that time I smiled back at her. I knew what she was saying. I knew that I was different from Karen and Mark. I didn't want to talk to her about death, so I changed the subject to something else.

She encouraged me to take the job in Ireland. She told me that there was a time in her life when she wanted to visit that country. It was after she had married my grandfather. He had worked many years at a mine in Henderson, Colorado. They had a friend who was Irish, and they would sit for hours talking to him and listening to his Irish brogue.

She told me that my eyes were her eyes, and she could look through a window into the very soul of me. She said that she knew what I wanted to say or think before I did. She was more than a grandmother to me, she was a huge part of my being! She then put cookie dough on the end of my nose and we laughed and joked about everything.

I had to stop thinking about the past and return to what was happening that day. The funeral car stopped in front of my parents' home. I turned my head and looked at my family. Karen was wiping her eyes and nose. She continued to sob while her husband, Ted, held her hand and tried his best to comfort her and wipe away the tears that filled her eyes. There was no way that anyone could stop the pain that was running through our hearts, not just that day, but for the rest of our lives.

Mark was staring out the window with his pipe firmly in his mouth. He, too, was trying not to show his true emotions. He had a sick idea that a real man never cries. When he didn't think anyone was watching, a tear drop would fall from his eyes.

My mother's head was resting snugly on my father's shoulder. She had a soft smile on her lips. I could tell that she, too, was thinking about Grandmother.

After all of us had climbed out of the funeral car, my father wrapped his arms around my mother's waist. Ted held Karen, and Mark walked with me into our house. In our minds at that time, we all felt as if life would never be the same without our precious grandmother there to lead the way for all of us.

As we entered the house I noticed that the mirror in the entrance way was tilted. I went over to straighten it. As I looked at the glass I saw what I believed to be an apparition of Grandmother staring back at me! I thought that maybe my imagination was making me see something that I wanted to see one more time.

When I looked back at the mirror, the apparition had vanished! I wanted to tell my family what I thought I saw. Instead, I decided to wait until another time and place.

My father took my mother into the living room to rest. Karen kept telling Ted how she should have spent more time with Grandmother, and Mark stood at the fireplace, puffing on his pipe. He still looked very distant.

After dinner I told everyone that I was leaving. When I left, I drove to Grandmother's home, in hopes of seeing her again. As I drove down the interstate I could feel the wind blowing my hair against my face.

After I arrived at her home, I parked in the driveway and walked to the back of the house. Under the WELCOME mat was a spare key. I let myself in. On the shelf inside the back door were candles that she kept in case of an emergency. I took a match and lit one. Then I walked through the house and up the stairs to her bedroom.

As I stood there looking around the room, I saw many things that reminded me of Grandmother. I walked over to a stool in front of her big dresser mirror that I knew so well. That was the place where she would sit to brush her long hair. We had spent many hours in there, talking.

When I gazed into the mirror, I saw an image start to appear and it was the image of Grandmother. She had come back once more to visit me. I looked at her eyes and said, "Grandmother, what is it that you want to say to me?"

I thought that some way she would speak to me and I could hear her voice again. I waited to hear her talk to me. I heard nothing.

At that moment I realized that there was only one way that I could communicate with her. That would be for me to use the one thing that we both shared. That certain thing was called our "Mind Power."

I looked deep into her eyes and listened with my mind. I could hear her say, "Amy, my darling granddaughter, I have come back to you, to tell you that our family is in horrible danger! When you were small, your mother and father told you the story about their trip to Henderson, Colorado. I'm not sure you believed them. What they told you about is true!

"When they left there, they thought they had destroyed all of the evil that was down in the old

Henderson Mine. Later, when they had returned to L.A. at the time of their wedding, your mother talked with her mind to a man who had been transformed into one of the creatures of the night. He liked your mother before he was killed, and never forgot about her, even in death. He told her that some of the evil ones had escaped! The one that was feared the most was not destroyed. He also escaped! He swore to get even with every member of our family. It is time now! They want the revenge that they didn't get at the time of the fire and explosion.

"What I am saying, Amy, is this ... the Nosferatu are back! Karen and Mark are too weak. They would only be at their mercy. Your mother and father are too old to fight them again. It is up to you now to save your family! If the time comes when you need help, Amy, you can bring me back to help you. Be brave, and don't trust anyone unless you know that they are safe!"

At that time, I watched Grandmother vanish. I stayed there on her stool, staring at the mirror, hoping she would return. She didn't.

I had known all my life that I was different from Karen and Mark. I was born with mental telepathy. I guess that is why I can communicate with other people without them knowing it. Also, I was blessed with what my grandmother and my mother called "Mind Power." All three of us shared it. With this power I can control objects in a manner that would benefit myself or a purpose. Up until that time in my life, I had found no need to use this power, but after hearing my grandmother's words to me, I knew that it was up to me to protect my family from the outrageous creatures of the night.

2

VISIT FROM
UNEXPECTED VISITORS

The moment had passed and I could see that Grandmother wasn't coming back. In front of me were many items that were special to her. She had old pictures on the walls of our family. On the night stand was a locket that my grandfather had given her just a few weeks before he was killed. Inside it was a picture of Grandmother and Mother. She wore it often, saying that she thought it gave her good luck.

I picked up the locket and put it around my neck. I knew that she would want me to wear it always, and to this day I still do.

On the shelf next to the bed was a gold music box. When Karen was small, Grandmother would open it and play the song for her. I would give that to Karen. Each object that I touched brought back memories for me. Even though I knew Grandmother was no longer in the room, I felt like she would watch over me always.

There was nothing left for me to do in her home, so I walked down the stairs and to her front door, blowing out the candle when I got ready to leave. While standing there, I turned my head to look one last time at everything that surrounded me, knowing that I would never forget the memories that were stored in that house.

After I returned to my home, I could see that someone had been there! The front door was left cracked open, and the lock appeared to be broken.

Quietly, I opened the door and softly entered the room. I wasn't sure if who or what could still be inside waiting for me.

I turned on the lights and started walking back to my living room. There, in the middle of the floor, was a puddle of blood! I remember thinking that if Grandmother was right, the Nosferatu had been there, and they had left a message for me! They were telling me that if I went to find them, the next puddle of blood would be none other than my own.

That night I could hardly sleep. I kept hoping that my mind would tell me where they could be found. Even if it did, I knew that the Nosferatu that was their leader would leave the rest of them. In order for me to make everything safe for my family, I had to destroy the leader first!

As the night progressed, I still found it hard to sleep. I got out of bed and went to my desk. Inside was my grandfather's old journal that he used when he was a miner in the small town of Henderson, Colorado. I opened it and read several pages that were filled with his thoughts.

While reading it, I saw a section that I had overlooked. It read, "Those that destroy, destroy themselves! There's no turning back!" Somehow the Nosferatu must have told my grandfather that the day they saw him down in the mine.

When my mother and father destroyed a lot of them, they jeopardized the life of our family. Not knowing this is why we were still in danger. My biggest question was, is my mind strong enough to do this?

In the morning I went back to my parents' home. Karen and Ted were already there. She had found out that she and Ted were going to be parents. This was all the more reason for me to find the right way to protect my family.

My brother Mark was still very quiet. He never was a man with many words, but I could see that something was bothering him, and it was time to find out what it was. "Mark, are you all right? The last few days you have been quieter than usual. Is there something going on that I should know about?"

Mark looked at me with a sad look and said, "I'm all right. At least where Grandmother is concerned. She was an old woman and was going to pass on sooner or later. I'm sorry she died, but I'm not surprised. I have just been standing here, thinking about you, Amy. You are my baby sister and I hate to see you go so far away from us. I know that this is your decision and that you need your own space. I just wish that there was something that I could say or do to change your mind."

I told him that I was sorry that he was so sad, and that I would come back to L.A. as often as I could. Also, not to worry about me as I would be fine. I also told Mark that I would miss all of them, but that there was something that I had to do and that someday he would understand. At that time, a tear ran down my face.

As I was hugging Mark, I looked at my father, who also looked very solemn. I walked over to him and said, "Hi, Dad! How is it going? Is Mom feeling better? How are you holding up?"

My father looked up at me and said, "How's my little princess doing? I am doing fine. As for Mother, she has gone to her favorite place to think. I can see that there is something bothering her, but she won't tell me what it is. She just says that she needs to talk to you. Maybe you can find out what it is that is hurting her inside so much."

I told my dad that I would have her back to smiling in no time, after I kissed him on the cheek.

On my way down to the beach to speak to Mother, I took off my shoes. I could see her staring out at the water and smiling, like she had been yesterday when we were all on our way back here after the funeral. There was something she was thinking about that was making her feel happy. I sat down beside her and listened to what she had to say.

Grandmother had also paid her a visit the night she passed away, and told her what she had told me. She told me the story again about their adventure, not only in the town of Henderson, but also at the old Henderson Mine. She also informed me that the Nosferatu were more modern than years ago and could look human one minute and like a creature from the night the next. Also, what I would need to do to destroy them, and to be careful who I chose to trust.

Mother also told me that if I needed her, she would come there to help me, as well as Grandmother would. After Mother and I had spoken and played in the sand for a while, I stood up and walked away.

Over the next several weeks I did what I needed to do to draw them to me. With my mind I would talk to them and I knew they heard me. I could smell a sour odor of rotting skin and at times death in the room. I knew there was nowhere I could hide from the creatures of the night.

3

HIDING
AND WATCHING

I knew that they could hear me speak to them through my mind as the room shook and the floor would buckle up around me.

Finally the day came when I took a taxi to my mother and father's home. Everyone was there to take me to the airport, where I would pursue my venture to Ireland, to work in a hospital and do my best to destroy the creatures.

Mother once again reminded me of the danger that I was in as she had felt their demon for a few weeks. I told Mother that if I needed her to join me, I would call her, but to stay calm and try not to worry about me. We all said our goodbyes with many tears running down our faces as that could have been the last time that we saw each other. I hugged them and walked away. My new destination would be Limerick, Ireland, where I have made my home ever since that day.

When I arrived here, I met a man who eventually would become my husband for the rest of his and my life. His name is Clark Allen. He was the Chief Administrator of the hospital in Limerick. It took me a while to trust him, or anyone there, because of the words spoken by my grandmother and my mother. When I looked around, everyone looked normal, and this was deceiving as my mother had told me it would be.

There was a lot of devastation that took place there that started shortly after my arrival. An old woman had passed away who shouldn't have. A train derailed, leaving many people dead, with some of them coming back to life as creatures of the night. A nurse who looked normal was spotted by me, eating the flesh and drinking the blood from dead bodies in the basement, along with others that were doing the same thing.

There was what was referred to as a Chief Administrator there by the name of Steve Weston, who had worked in the hospital five years ago, until his car went off the road and he was killed. There was also a mention about a woman administrator who didn't exist. I found out that I could trust a young girl by the name of Alice Palmer, who came there to the hospital to visit her grandmother, who shouldn't have been there in the first place. When we found her, she had little holes in her neck, where she had been bitten by the creatures.

The Nosferatu were killing innocent people again, just like they had done for many years, not only in Germany but also in Henderson, Colorado, and in Ireland.

I had told Alice and Clark the story that was told to me, and Clark was still confused about some of it, so I explained more in depth to him what was going on.

The bodies in the morgue were disappearing and the people from the morgue in town were confused as to how a dead body could up and walk out of the hospital.

One morning I was awakened by a scratching noise coming from outside my cottage. It sounded like it might be coming from my front door. I got up out of bed, slipped on my slippers and walked out of my bedroom. I went down the stairway to see what was making the sound.

When I opened my door, I saw an older dog. He was a tan color with white around each paw. He looked like he was half collie and half German shepherd. He also looked like he hadn't been fed. I bent down and stroked his back, to let him know that I was friendly and wouldn't hurt him. He licked my face and hand, and showed me that he needed a home and a friend to take care of him. I looked for a tag, to see if he belonged to anyone. There was none. From that day on, he would belong to me.

Since I didn't know what his name was, I decided to call him Nemo. That was the name of my dog when I was a small child. He was with me all the time until the day that someone hit him in the street with their car and he died.

Nemo followed me everywhere that I went, and we were becoming good friends.

Clark and I were becoming closer, and he was the one person there besides Amy whom I did trust. He had asked me to go to his parents' home to meet his mother, father and little sister. I accepted his invitation. Every one of them were very nice and his sister loved Nemo. They also became good friends.

When we left their home, we drove into town to the hospital. Clark asked me if I wanted to go inside, and I told him no, that I would wait for him in the car. Nemo acted jittery and I felt very uncomfortable. I knew that we weren't alone. The car started shaking and I heard a hissing sound outside. Nemo lunged at the car window and barked fiercely. The car was rocking back and forth. I was very happy when Clark returned to the car as I was worried that the Nosferatu were going to kill him.

On the way to the hospital the next day, I was straightening my rear-view mirror when I saw someone following me. The car would turn the same direction that I would turn. I drove faster in hopes of leaving the person behind me. No matter what I did, the person in the car did the same. There was an old highway up ahead that I had never driven on. I knew that this was my only hope of getting away from whomever was following me.

I turned off the main road and started up the old highway. On one side of it was a cliff. On the other, a ditch. At times I would be driving so fast that my car would squeal around a sharp turn. I looked in the mirror to see if the car was close to me, and when I looked back at the highway, I saw a guard rail in front of me. I slammed on my brakes. My car was skidding and sliding! All I could do was turn the wheel toward the ditch and hope that I wouldn't go over the cliff instead.

When I had come to a complete stop, my car was sitting in the ditch. I had just missed going over the cliff! I tried to start the car. It wouldn't start. I looked around to see if the person who had been following me was in sight. Whoever it was had vanished! I tried to open my door, but it was stuck.

All I knew was that I had to get out of there right away as I was a sitting duck for the creatures, if they were following me. I crawled out the window and started walking down the old highway, not knowing who to trust if anyone stopped to pick me up.

I saw a car coming down the highway. I kept walking slowly, fearful of whom might be in the car. When the car stopped, it turned out to be a nice old man who told me that it looked to him like I had gotten myself into a mess. If he only knew the other half of it. When he offered me a ride into town, I told him that I appreciated it, and he continued to talk, telling me how he drove a milk truck on that highway every day. I told him that I was a doctor in the hospital and about what I had experienced on the highway to lead me to the ditch.

The old man asked me if I was all right, as there were no guard rails on that highway. He said that I must have dozed off and dreamt it. I knew I wasn't asleep at the wheel of my car, and seeing a café up ahead, I asked him to drop me off there. I then called Clark to come and get me. The old man told me that it would be a good idea not to take that highway again because of all the animals that come out at night, and the waitress inside the café was telling me the same thing. She also told me that the highway used to be well traveled until the mine up ahead had closed, and that the owner of the café was shutting down the café, since there was little business any longer.

Soon Clark came and I was ready to leave. I had a lot to tell him. I told him what the waitress said about the old mine that had been closed a couple of months ago. She even said that she thought she saw a ghost looking back at her one night when she was working late. She remarked that it had blood-stained teeth. She believes that it was just her imagination working overtime, and after she ran out of the café to leave, her boss offered her more money to stay. So she accepted it.

I wanted to tell her that what she saw was real and that it was a Nosferatu looking at her, getting ready to make a kill. I believed that the old man might know where they were staying during the time when they weren't changing how they really looked. I didn't know if she would have believed me. Now that I knew about the mine and the creatures that are in Limerick,

I knew that I wasn't going to be satisfied until I had come back out there to try to find the mine that she was talking about.

There had to be a connection. Even though the Nosferatu were modern and could change in an instant, looking human and not like creatures, I knew that they still felt the need to go back to their roots. The cave in Germany and the old Henderson Mine were the places where they first took their human form. The horrible-looking creature that the waitress saw that night was real! Just like every Nosferatu, which are also referred to as vampires, they work and eat at night and are more than likely asleep in the mine during the day. I was hoping that there would be a way to get rid of them without entering the mine.

Clark asked me if I knew the name of the mine, and I told him no. I also mentioned that we could go back out to the cafe later on that night, to speak to the waitress who could tell us.

When we arrived at the hospital that day, I went to a room of a young man who had been injured in the factory fire. I will never forget the words that he spoke to me.

"I was very afraid when the fire first started. All the workers were scattered in different areas of the factory. My job was to use a forklift to stack the items. That night there were some strange men who came in to see our boss. Apparently he knew that they were coming. He said to let them into his office. He then asked to see the workers, one by one. No one knew why they were asked to go in there. When they returned, they couldn't remember why they were there or what was said to them.

"I was on my way in when some crates fell down.

I went over there to fix them. When I was through, I was on my way in to see what they wanted when the men came out of the office. Everything was running fine until the men were there. After a while, one of the workers smelled smoke. He yelled, 'FIRE!' and everyone started running to the door to leave. The door would not open! Before long, the smoke was so thick in there that it was hard to see. Everyone was running and yelling for help! Some of us managed to escape through a small opening in the basement that wasn't sealed very good. We called for assistance right away.

"When I looked, I saw men and women with their faces pressed tightly up against the windows. They were frantic with fear! They were pounding on each window, begging for someone to help them! The windows wouldn't break so they could escape the clutches of the fire that was spreading with intensity throughout the factory. I stood there and watched the ones inside lose their fight for their lives when the fire exploded into horrifying flames!

"There was nothing that I or anyone else could do. Soon the screams stopped and the night was silent and still."

Even today this story of this brave young man gives me chills. He and Alice Palmer were lucky to be alive.

I told the young man that I needed to check his neck for injury. The truth was that I needed to check for fang marks! I saw none. He was all right.

In the next room, there was a body of an older woman who hadn't been as lucky. She had died during the night. The orderly had covered her up with the sheet. I took it off and looked over her body. Just like the other people who had died, she had fang marks on her neck. There were holes from the creatures that were similar to those who had died before her.

I was certain that there were more creatures downstairs. This time I wasn't leaving until I found the one that was claiming his kill!

I sent a note to Clark. It said that I had something important to do. I told him to go back to the café, to talk to the waitress.

I walked quietly down the stairs. I could hear at that moment that there was someone in the morgue and I didn't want to be seen. When I had reached the bottom, I hid in a crevice in the basement, large enough to hide me. I sat there, watching to see who the person was that would be coming out of the room.

After a few minutes, a tall man walked out. When he passed me, I could see that it was the janitor who worked at night in the ward where I worked, on the same floor every night. He had come there to eat the flesh and drink the blood of those lying there on a table. There were dark red drippings from his chin. His eyes were wild. He was pale and his teeth were stained red. I was trying very hard not to get into his mind. I didn't want him to find me.

The janitor put his head back and hissed with delight. He had just drank the blood of his choice for the night. Now he would go back to work.

I was trying to get out of the crevice when I heard another noise. It was the sound of a woman coming out of the morgue. She was the one that the janitor had bitten once again. She, too, was one of the walking dead! I watched her walk up the stairs and out the side door used by the people who came to the hospital to identify their dead family and friends.

When I knew that I was safe, I climbed out of the crevice and walked back up the stairs. Now that I knew that the janitor was one of the evil creatures, I had to find a way to stop him!

I was sure that he, too, had left the hospital to go back to the mine. The sun would be coming up before long. The only thing left for me to do was to go back to Clark's office and wait for him to return.

What I didn't know at that time and about Clark was that while I was in the basement, he too was having some real problems!

After Clark had left for the cafe to talk to the waitress, he was driving down the deserted highway. He was driving slowly and watching ahead of the car. At times animals would run across the road in front of him. They looked like they were running from something that was walking around. Clark was playing the radio and watching the connecting roads. He wanted to make sure that he turned off on the right one.

Suddenly, from out of nowhere a man jumped from behind a big rock toward Clark's car! He tried to startle Clark into stopping. Instead, Clark swerved in hopes of missing the man. He didn't succeed. The car hit him and knocked him to the side of the highway.

Clark stopped and went over to see if the man might be alive. By the time he had gotten over there, the man's facial appearance had changed. He was old and ugly! He had turned into the creature. Clark ran back to his car and left before the man could hurt him.

Clark had found the right road to the cafe. As he drove, he saw people sitting in their fields, eating off of cows that were dead. Blood was seeping out the corners of their mouths and dripping from their faces! Their hands were red and full of bloody meat! Clark was afraid that they, too, would charge his car. He had entered a community of Nosferatu.

As he got closer to the cafe, he had a feeling that something wasn't right. The lights were on inside the cafe and the front door was wide open. He got out of his car and walked up to the cafe, looking around at everything. The place was very quiet. The waitress was nowhere around the area.

Clark went inside and walked over to a stool at the counter. He sat there, waiting for her to return. He had only been sitting there for a minute, knowing that it was strange that the front door would be open. He got up and walked to the kitchen, the bathrooms and the storage room, looking for her.

He was about to give up and leave when he noticed that the door to the freezer was open. He went there to look in and saw blood on the floor around the opening. He completely opened the door and saw her hanging from a meat hook. She had been skinned alive! The creatures had found her and eaten all of the meat from her bones.

He turned around and ran out to his car. He locked the doors and drove away. After he returned, he told me what he had seen and experienced. From that moment on, we decided that we would sleep during the day as with everything that we both had discovered, we were on our way to finding out who the leader was.

4

THE BASEMENT

The clock on the wall in Clark's office was reading 4:00 A.M. It was time to talk to Alice Palmer before going home.

We drove to the country. She lived a few miles out of town. It was early when we arrived at her home, and I wasn't sure she would be awake.

When we reached her home, we saw lights on. We knocked. Soon after, she answered the door. Alice asked us to sit down and said that she didn't expect company that early.

I told her that we were sorry to bother her, but that I had some important questions to ask her about the night of the factory explosion, and was hoping that she could answer them. When I asked her about that night, this is what she told us:

"I was standing at the long table that was used to stack the candles when they came off of the relay belt. I was putting them into boxes when I saw some new people walk past me. There was something different about them. The men had light complexions and didn't talk to anyone. When they came into the factory, they walked past us and went into Mr. Thompson's office. He was our boss. They never knocked on his door. Instead, they walked in and shut the door behind them. For some reason, the workers were told to come into his office, one at a time. When they returned, they couldn't remember what was said to them in there.

"I went to the bathroom to wash my hands. While I was in there, I heard someone yell out that the factory was on fire. I climbed onto the sink and pulled myself up to an open window. That is when I escaped. I could hear the people in there, screaming. The fire was spreading fast and no one could open any doors! When I reached the ground, I saw where some of the other workers had gotten out like I did, so we went for help. Not too long after that is when the ambulance and the fire trucks showed up.

"There was something else that happened before the men left the factory. There is a nurse that works with you. I've seen her in the hospital a few times. She walked past me and was only in there for a short time. When she came out, she appeared to be in a hurry. We all laughed and said that she was probably late for work. Shortly after that is when the men came out of Mr. Thompson's office and left the factory."

I asked Alice if the nurse was young and pretty and was told that her name tag was Nurse Adams. It was clear to me then that I had no choice but to believe that she was mixed up with the creatures of the night, or was one of them herself.

Clark and I thanked Alice for her time and left. From there we drove to my cottage. Nemo was waiting patiently for me to return. He was happy to see us. Before Clark left, he told me that he would come back to get me just before dark.

The hours in the day passed and it was nighttime. I had fed Nemo, and when Clark arrived we left for the hospital. I was going to watch Nurse Adams. I had to see where she went at night while she was there to work.

That day, Alice had given Clark directions to the old mine that was close to the cafe. He went there to watch the area.

After Clark let me out at the hospital, I observed Nurse Adams standing there, doing her usual nothing. I told her that I needed the charts of some of the patients. This was my excuse that I gave her in order to stand there and wait for her to leave, so that I could follow her.

Eventually she left and walked to the door leading downstairs to the basement. There was a door barely cracked and I could see what she was doing in there.

What I saw made me sick! She was in the room where the patients that had died were taken to, so that doctors could do an autopsy. She took a knife and slit open a man. She put both of her hands inside the body. Her head was pointed and bald. She had black circles under her eyes and she was pale. Her teeth had become fangs and she was sipping the blood from the insides of the man.

As I suspected, she too was a creature of the night. Now that I knew that she was one of them, I was wondering how many more of these evil creatures worked in the hospital.

I watched until she had her fill, and her face and head changed back to a human form. She wiped the blood from her mouth and lips and walked back up the stairs to the second floor. I then went into the lounge to wait for Clark to return.

Meanwhile, Clark was getting close to the old mine. The air was still and smelled sour, like rotting flesh. There was a stench like nothing he had ever smelled before. It was the smell of death!

Clark parked off the road, where he could sit in his car to watch the mine. He sat there for some time, watching and waiting. What he did see coming from there was not human! This was where he knew for sure that the creatures had been staying during the day, only to come out at night.

He started his car and left. As he drove back on the same road, he noticed a colony of creatures feasting on the blood of cows.

After Clark parked his car, he ran through the parking lot to the hospital. He took the elevator to the second floor and after the elevator had stopped and he got out of it, he ran down the hall to the room where I was waiting for him. He couldn't wait to tell me what he had discovered at the mine.

I, too, told him about Nurse Adams. We knew that we were moving forward in the right direction.

5

ANOTHER TIME
AND PLACE

Clark and I were getting closer to the truth. With all of that, though, I still had no idea who the leader was. Without that knowledge, my family and I were still in danger.

I remember how we felt at that time back then, and all of the anticipation waiting to happen, not knowing from one move to another whether we would both be killed by the creatures.

We were on our way to the cafeteria when I was sure that I saw Doctor Weston again. It looked like he was going into the main part of the hospital. I stopped walking and said, "Clark, I just saw Steve Weston."

Clark asked me if I was sure and reminded me that he had showed me his grave. I assured him that my eyes weren't playing tricks on me, and that he had gone to the lobby. At first I know that Clark had doubts, but then he agreed that we should follow him.

We walked down the hall to the corridor, which led to the lobby in the main part of the hospital. When we stepped around the corner of the room, for some unknown reason we had crossed over into another time and another place.

I looked at Clark. His appearance was different! He was dressed in a plaid business suit. He had a narrow mustache, much like those worn by men back in the 1920s.

I looked at myself. I had a simple house dress on. My hair was pulled back from my face and was piled on top of my head. I was wearing laced boots that ran halfway up my legs.

People were walking around us, going in different directions, doing many things. I looked at a calendar that was on a nearby desk. It read August 14, 1924. We were no longer in our time period.

Someone was trying to tell us something. Whoever it was did not belong in our world! I followed Clark into a room that looked like it had charts and records of the people who were in there.

On the wall was a picture of a man that resembled Steve Weston. We were sure that he must be a close relative of his.

This was our first clue. We looked through every record until we came to one that said Sam Weston. Clark opened the file and read to me what was written down. The paper was old and yellow with age. The ink was faded and outdated, but Clark could still read what it said. He sat down beside me and read Sam's medical records. This was what we found out that day.

In the month of July, Sam was admitted into the hospital. He had been complaining of a sore neck. The doctor in charge admitted him right away. His diagnosis was a pinched nerve. The doctor said that Sam would only be in the hospital for a short time. Weeks went by and he never got better.

His grandson became worried about him. One day, when he went back to the hospital to see the doctor who was taking care of his grandfather, he found out that his grandfather had passed away the night before! The diagnosis showed that there was nothing wrong with the old man's heart or his back. Instead, the doctor who did the autopsy found piercing marks that were made from fangs on Sam's neck! His neck was bruised. The date that he died was August 14, 1924. That was the same date on the calendar in the lobby!

Clark looked through the records for something else. The records and the notations that had been written down and placed in the file with the records was the only way that we knew what had taken place during that period of time before Sam had passed away. Someone other than the doctor, at that time, had written down the story so that the truth would be known in the future.

This was the only thing Clark found that day that might have been the reason why we were brought there. Doctor Weston wanted us to know that Mary Palmer was like his grandfather! She went to the hospital for something that could have been treated at home! Doctor Weston knew this! Before he could help her escape from her room, the creatures killed her as they did his grandfather.

I knew now that he wasn't the doctor after all who had admitted her as we were made to believe. The doctor that Alice and Mary saw wasn't a doctor at all! It had to have been the janitor pretending to be the doctor. The administrator that was there could have been none other than Nurse Adams, and Alice somehow forgot to make the connection the night of the factory explosion and all the times that she had gone to the hospital to visit her grandmother.

After Clark had put the records back in the drawer and we walked out of the room, I saw Doctor Weston smiling at me, and then he vanished. He could rest in peace now that the truth was known. I also knew then that, back then, Henderson, Colorado wasn't the only place that the Nosferatu had chosen to make their new home. They had picked Limerick, Ireland as well.

After leaving that room, we were back in our own time and place. When we left the hospital that day, we went back to the grave of Doctor Weston, where I laid flowers across his tombstone. Clark looked at the date on it and it also said August 14. Steve Weston had been killed on the same day that his grandfather had died!

From there we returned to my cottage to stay the rest of the night. As we stood in the middle of the living room, the floor started jumping and the floorboards spread apart in hopes of swallowing us whole! The ceiling shook and the lights flicked on and off. The windows flew open and a strong wind filled the room with a cold air. The small objects moved around until they fell to the floor. The pictures on the wall shifted from one side to the other. It was as if a great earthquake was starting!

What we had felt hadn't come from Mother Nature. It was a warning for me! I was getting close to knowing what the creatures didn't want me to know. I knew that what I was up against was a powerful force that had every intention of killing me and everyone close to me that dared to get in their way!

When the darkness was near, it was time for us to go to the one place where we knew the walking creatures gathered to eat and take the dead that had become one of them.

We were on our way to the Nosferatu community so that I could bring them all together in one place.

That day I made Nemo stay behind again. I wasn't sure if Clark and I were going to make it out of there alive, and I couldn't risk Nemo's life as well.

We drove to the place where Clark had seen dead cows rotting. The vampires would go back there to eat and drink blood. Clark parked the car in a place where tall trees, being blown around by the wind, made it difficult for us to be seen. There we watched for them.

Time passed and many of the creatures were coming from all directions to take part in some kind of a ceremony. They were wearing black robes with large hoods that covered their faces. They had all gathered together to drink blood from a large bottle. Each time a drink was taken, the Nosferatu would rear their ugly heads and hiss and growl in delight! Their faces were so deformed from their transformation, Clark and I couldn't tell who they were.

More and more came to partake in the blood feast that was for their pleasure.

Hours passed. There still was no sign of the leader. I knew that I couldn't wait any longer. It was time for me to summon him.

I told Clark to leave me there and go back home. I didn't want him to be in any danger. He refused to go, saying that he felt destined to be with me, either in this life or another.

At that moment I kissed him and stood up so that the creatures could see me. I walked straight ahead toward them. While walking, I stared out into the darkness. "With my mind, I told the leader to join me. I wanted him to come to me.

From the darkness came a tall man walking toward me. He was wearing a dark cloak that covered his body. This was the moment I had been waiting for.

Clark also stood up and walked over to me. As I looked at the man in red, my mind was simultaneously mixed with his.

As he walked up to me, he said, "I was wondering when you would beckon me to come to you. For many years now I have waited for this day. I was in the old Henderson Mine when your mom and dad destroyed a lot of my family. You see, to you, Amy, we are just monsters, beasts or ghouls. We are Nosferatu! That of one family! We enjoy eating the flesh of the humans that we are attracted to. Instead of killing you, Amy, I want you to join us. I want you to be a member of our family throughout eternity! You will be able to do whatever you want to do forever!"

My answer to him was, "I thought that you would come to me. I waited and then after I found out more about your kind, I decided that I had waited long enough. I will not let you hurt or kill any of my family! I will not join you! I would rather be dead than look and act like you!"

At that moment the Nosferatu took their hoods off. They had changed themselves into human form. Everyone that I had worked with at the hospital was standing there in front of me! They, too, were creatures of the night!

Nurse Adams walked over to the leader. She tilted her head back and laughed in a shrill way. She had gotten the last word with me.

I looked at each one of them and said, "It's time for me to do what I came here to do."

At that time, I looked at a pile of branches that were lying on the ground. I focused my mind on it. It started burning! The flames rose higher and higher. The leader became mad and outraged with me.

They reached for Clark and me. We started running toward the fire. Behind it we thought that we would be safe. I was wrong! The Nosferatu came closer and closer to us. I waited until they were real close and then I looked at the fire and told it with my mind to rise up and strike the creatures that were near.

The fire raised up and lashed out at the Nosferatu. They started howling and hissing at us. They were on fire and burning! The others stepped back from the flames.

More and more of them kept coming, and soon we were surrounded by hundreds of them. They could smell our blood and wanted to eat our flesh, too. Their faces were old and ugly once again.

I looked at them and told them to follow me into the nearby lake. Then the leader told me that they would not listen to me. He said that there was no way that Clark and I would make it out of there alive.

I looked at him and said, "Don't be too sure of that!" I knew that they were hungry and that they never gave up on anyone they wanted. I knew that the leader was wrong. They would follow me. They wanted to partake of my blood and flesh!

Clark and I started running toward the lake. There was no way that we could fight all of them standing there. They followed us as I was certain they would. The faster we ran, the more determined they were to kill us, just like they did the wild animals that they had made to become their prey.

Before we reached the lake, we saw the old mine that they inhabited. This was the place where I could get them together in one place. I had to make sure that I killed the leader and that none of them escaped as they had at the old Henderson Mine.

Clark kept asking me if I was sure of what I was doing. He said that in the mine there was no way that we would make it out of there alive. He said that we had never been in there before. I assured him that I had to get all of them together inside there, to be able to destroy not just the leader but *all* of them.

We walked down the portal inside the mine, watching in front and behind us. We even crawled when we had to. We had reached a narrow part of the mine. Below us was a mast that led to a large body of water that had found its way into the mine.

Carefully we got down on our knees and crawled to the other side. There were bones and dead animals that had been eaten, lying everywhere!

Clark and I could hear them coming. They were wanting to stop us before I stopped them. At the top of the cave was light. I had to find a way to bring them all together in that one area. When I knew that there was no more of them waiting outside, I would open the top of the mine and let the light shine in there on them.

Clark and I continued to climb upward. While climbing, rocks and debris fell to the ground. I reached for a place to put my hand. The leader told the formation to close. It did and I could feel my feet slipping from the crevice that I was standing on. The leader was climbing up the rocks to destroy us—as we wanted to destroy them.

My foot slipped and Clark grabbed my hand. He pulled me up to where he was. I took another step up to a ledge that was close to the opening. The leader was getting closer to us.

As I stepped upward, the leader grabbed my foot. I wasn't going anywhere! It was all I could do to keep from falling to my death.

He was hanging tightly onto my ankle. There was nothing I could do to stop him. My ankle was getting numb from the pain and my hands were starting to sweat. Clark kept reaching for me.

Then the leader said to me, "Amy, you should know better than to try to escape from me. I told you that there was no way that you would remain alive in here, or any place else. I will kill you myself and let my family below feast on your body! That is ... unless you've changed your mind about becoming one of us," he added with great intensity.

I couldn't look at him to use my mind power! There was only one last hope that I had. I remembered that if I needed her, Grandmother would come back to me. Now I knew that I had no choice! My hand was slipping and I knew that I didn't have much time. I took my locket in my hand and said, "Grandmother, I have never needed you before like I do now. Please come back to me and help me fight this creature!" I kept clutching the locket between my fingers.

Suddenly, I could see a streak of light coming past me with a flash! I knew that Grandmother was there and that she would help me destroy the leader.

I could hear what she was telling me. "Amy, reach for the moss that is growing out of the rock. I will keep it from breaking. I heard your cry for help. I have never broken a promise to you. I will never let the Nosferatu hurt or kill you."

At that moment I did what she told me to do, and I was able to hang on. The leader also heard what Grandmother told me. He let go of my ankle and started back down the rocks. He looked deeply into her eyes and she told him, "You should have been destroyed years ago! Now I will end your existence! You won't have to worry about eternity, you scum-bag! I will not let you kill anyone in my family! You are not strong enough to fight me!"

Grandmother told me to do what I had come there to do. She said that I had to use my mind power to destroy all of them.

I looked upward toward the top of the mine. I told Clark to hold on tightly to what he was holding onto, that he was going to think that the earth was going to open up.

He did what I said to do, and then I looked up again at the opening. I had to kill the leader first, so I told the top of the mine to let some light in.

Suddenly, the top of the mine started breaking up and pieces of it fell to the ground. The leader grabbed his face. The flesh started tearing away from the bone and falling to the bottom of the mine. The leader's foot slipped from the rock and he fell into the body of water that was in the mine below us. When he hit the water, steam came up and his skin melted from what was left of his body. He would never bother anyone again! The light was enough to destroy him.

The Nosferatu below us were yelling and screaming. Nurse Adams was begging for forgiveness and promising to change her ways if we would only spare her. Unfortunately for her, it was my turn for the last word.

I looked at her and said, "Go back to hell where you belong!" Then I told the opening to widen and let the light shine brightly down on us all.

The top of the mine opened wide and the light shone brighter than it had ever shone before. I could see each one of the creatures of the night fading away. They were hit by the sunlight pouring into the mine. The light had destroyed them all!

I looked at my grandmother and said, "Thank you for coming back here to help me. I couldn't have done it without you. I will always love you and I'll never forget you! Someday we will be together."

"You would have done fine without me, Amy. You have always done everything that you could do for all of us. You gave them the gift of life. Our family will be safe now. I love you, Amy! You have nothing more to fear. The Nosferatu will not be able to hurt or kill anyone ever again."

Once more I watched Grandmother vanish with the streak of light with which she came to me.

6

TRIP TO HENDERSON

Clark and I had climbed down from the rocks, and for the first time in a long while, I felt safe. The creatures were no longer there and, as far as we knew, no longer were in existence. My family could lead a normal life now.

There was something going on in my mind at that time that I couldn't stop thinking about. After the creatures left Henderson, Colorado, and came here to Ireland to live, in hopes of existing without the threat of harm, Grandmother was right about our family being safe from them. I had killed the leader of the creatures that were in the old Henderson Mine. If there were more of them out there somewhere, others would be at their mercy until they, too, could destroy them. I wasn't going to dwell on something that I wasn't sure about. Right now I was very happy to be alive and to have my whole life ahead of me.

After Clark and I had walked out into the beautiful sunshine that day and had driven to the hospital, Clark asked me to marry him. Of course I said yes as you already know. We called our families and told them the good news. I asked Mom when baby Steve had been born, and she told me August 14th. This was the reason that Doctor Steve Weston wouldn't hurt us. He knew that soon he would be a part of my family. He was reborn on the day that he had died in another life!

The wedding was beautiful. We would be staying in Limerick. When the wedding reception ended, I hugged my family and told them that I was happy that I didn't let them down, and told them that Clark and I would visit L.A. There were many tears that day, and Clark and I kept our promise as we made several trips there to be with our family.

Clark and I had said our goodbyes to all of my family and his. It was time for us to leave. The same thing happened to me just before the honeymoon that had happened to my mother when she and my father got ready to leave for theirs. At her wedding, she had seen Jack Winters watching and talking to her.

I also saw someone. The one person that I wanted most to be at my wedding was! My precious grandmother had returned to throw me a kiss for good luck. My day and life from that day forward was filled with many blessings.

As I was still sitting at the kitchen table, looking out my window, I remembered how handsome Clark looked that day. Our life that we shared was filled with so much joy and happiness.

Mother and Father have passed away now, and so has Clark. We created many memories and beautiful children that grew up and had children of their own.

Today my granddaughter, Maggie, and I were going to board a plane that would take us to a place where my story began many generations ago with my family.

Maggie had inherited the same gift that I did, and as far as I knew, she was the only one in my immediate family that had. I was all packed and waiting for her to knock on the door. I had my mother's journal that she had written many years ago about everything that was said and done before, during and after she and my father returned home. I had read it to Maggie before, but knowing her as well as I do, I was sure that she would want to hear the story again about the old Henderson Mine.

Every time that I looked at Maggie, I saw a much younger me looking back and smiling. She had graduated from law school and the trip back to Henderson, Colorado was my gift to her. Many times, while she was growing up, she told me that she wanted me to go with her back to the old town and visit the old Henderson Mine. So today, when we leave Ireland, I will be giving her the gift that she has wanted for years.

I heard a knock at the door and I knew that Maggie was here to get me. My bags were by the door and I was ready to leave.

I opened the door and heard, "Grandmother, I am so excited! Are you ready to leave?" Maggie commented.

"Yes, dear. I am all packed as you see, and ready to leave with you on our adventure," I replied.

"Then let's go have some fun!" she remarked.

We walked out to the car and were on our way to the airport. Our plane was on time and waiting for our arrival.

After we checked in and left our luggage, we were sitting, patiently waiting for them to let us know that we could board the plane. It was going to be a long flight, but one that I knew would give Maggie enjoyment and memories for the rest of her life.

Soon we heard that our plane was ready to board and we were walking down the corridor to enter the plane that would take us to Denver, Colorado, where I would rent a car to take us to the town of Henderson.

While seated, the plane left the ground, going upward into the clouds far above Earth. The flight attendant had come to us to give us something to drink, and we were watching out the window and talking. It wasn't long after that when Maggie asked me to read her the journal that her great-grandmother had written about Great-Grandfather's and her experience in Henderson, and all the rest of what took place before they went there and when they came back to L.A.

I told Maggie that I would be happy to read it to her again, in hopes that it didn't frighten the other passengers on the plane. At that moment, some of the passengers sitting around us said that they would love to hear a good story, and that it would make their time on the plane go quicker as well, so I started reading it, telling them to hang onto their seats as what I was reading was a true story, and that I was living proof of it. Even the flight attendant said that she would listen when she could and to please read the journal aloud.

Maggie was smiling, and so I started from the beginning of the journal, saying every word that was written loud enough so that everyone could hear the story, and this was what Mother wrote:

I love walking on the beach and watching the surf pound against the rocks. The wind is still and silent. The flowers are bright and full. The smell of lilac fills the air with a wonderful scent of freshness and beauty. It's a calm day in June. The smog has lifted and the sun is shining brighter than it has for several days. No matter where I go, the smell of the ocean will always be with me.

My name is Sarah Baker. I'm a news reporter for the *Ridgewood Times* newspaper in L.A. It's one of the largest newspapers in Southern California. I can truthfully say that I love working at this establishment.

Originally, I'm not a true native of California. I came here from a small mining town called Henderson, Colorado. The town sits on a hillside. It's surrounded by mountains and beautiful powder blue sky. Because the sky is so blue, whenever I lie on the ground, looking up toward Heaven, I feel as if I'm floating in the air, looking down on a large body of water below me. Sometimes during the day and night, the people in Henderson hear a coal train go rustling through the town on its way up the mountain to one of the remaining coal mines. There they pick up the coal and take it to the nearby cities for shipping.

Today, when I finally climbed out of bed, my objective was to find the nearest mirror in my bedroom. Today is my birthday. Like every woman in America, I wanted to see if I looked a year older. I checked for wrinkles and gray or white hair. I then took a shower and got ready for a glorious, fun-filled day. I was going to Santa Barbara to spend time with my brother, Danny, his wife Carla, and their family. My mother would be there also. She lives close by.

As I walked toward the front door to leave for the day, the phone rang. When I answered it, the voice on the other end was that of my boss, Frank Cooper.

"Sarah, sorry to bother you on your day off. I was sure that I would still catch you at home. It also gives me the opportunity to wish you a happy birthday! Are you still celebrating birthdays?" Frank said as he laughed heartily.

"Okay, Frank, we all know that I'm not getting younger with each passing year. We also know that I'm not an old lady either. I haven't reached the age where I choose not to get excited over my birthday each year," I told Frank skeptically. "What is the real reason you called me? You have never called me on the weekend unless there was something important that you wanted to talk to me about."

"You're right, Sarah. I would like you to go back

to your home town and do a story for the newspaper. You won't be going back there alone. I have asked Jim Peterson to go with you. The old Henderson Mine is going to reopen soon. A company from back East has bought it. The news media have been invited there to cover the story. Since the Henderson Mine was the most productive mine in the country, the market for its coal will be hot when it starts running. This is the biggest story to hit the front page in quite some time.

"Sarah, there is something else that I find hard to tell you about. There are a lot of strange things happening in Henderson now. Rumor is that some of the people passing through the area have seen what they believe to be apparitions walking around. All of this might be someone trying to scare away the people that have bought the old mine. Someone out there might not want it to reopen. I won't force you to go back there to do the assignment. You can think about it over the weekend and give me your answer Monday morning."

Frank was a very earnest man that wasn't afraid to express his feelings. He didn't get to be the boss sitting at his desk, clipping his toenails.

"I will give you an answer on Monday. My decision will require some serious thought. Thanks for calling, Frank."

"Goodbye, Sarah."

Ten years ago, the Henderson Mine caught on fire and several parts of it blew up. When the mine shut down, a lot of people lost their jobs. My dad was one of them. That was the reason why we moved to California.

Over the years I have tried to forget the sorrow on the faces of the families that lost their sons and husbands in the fire. It is wedged in my mind. I wasn't sure if I ever wanted to go back to Henderson.

I had a lot of thinking to do. I knew that Frank wouldn't fire me if I refused to go. Would I be letting myself down if I didn't go back there one more time? This was the question that hurt me all of my life. Then again, if the rumors were true, it could mean the end of my life!

7

UPSETTING NEWS

After Frank and I were finished with our conversation, I looked like a statue standing there with the phone still in my hand. I was dumbfounded, not knowing what to say or do. I was having one of those days when I wished I'd stayed in bed.

I put the phone down and grabbed the car keys. As I walked out the front door, I looked out at the ocean. The seagulls were landing in the sand on the beach. That was the place where they thought they belonged. Even though I had a good life before in Henderson, I had learned to love my life in Santa Monica, and my beach house. I knew that I would always feel that this is where I belonged.

The drive up the coast was beautiful. The air felt cool and refreshing.

When I drove into my brother Danny's driveway, I saw him with his chef's hat and apron on. His apron read: THE GRILL ISN'T THE ONLY PLACE I COOK. I saw Carla and Mom bringing food out from the house. My nephews were chosen to carry out the traditional birthday cake. This year there would be lots of little fingerprints in the frosting. The twins loved frosting. Next came baby Annie with my candles. It was time now for me to make my appearance known to my family.

"Sarah, we're so glad that you finally got here. Happy birthday!" Danny said as he accidentally burned his finger on the grill. He stood there, shaking it and trying real hard not to cuss around his children. Next to my dad, Danny was the best father in the world.

Mom came towards me to give me her birthday kiss, and Carla and the kids had lots of hugs for me also. It was great being there again.

While we sat there, eating hamburgers, Danny looked over at me. He said in a soft voice, "Sarah, you are awful quiet tonight. Is there something that you want to talk to me about?" Danny had taken over the role of father since Dad was found dead. He always loved me, but now he felt like he had to give me advice on everything that I did.

"You always could tell when I needed to talk. Today, before I left home, I received a call from my boss. He asked me to go back to Henderson and do a story on the reopening of the old Henderson mine. A company from the East bought it and they have asked us to come there. Frank told me something that has upset me. Apparently someone is trying to scare off anyone that gets within a hundred miles of the town or the mine. He said that tourists have reported seeing ghosts. I don't believe in ghosts and neither does Frank. There is someone that doesn't want the mine to reopen. They will stop at nothing to keep it from happening. Frank has given me until Monday to decide if I want to take the assignment. I won't be going alone. Frank has asked Jim Peterson to go with me. There is a chance that we could be in some real danger," I quietly told Danny, so that Mom wouldn't hear us talking.

Danny scooted his chair closer to mine and quietly said, "Sarah, I have always been proud of you, so I don't want you to misunderstand what I am about to say to you. I will always worry about you. You are my baby sister. I love you, but I don't like the job that you have. I have known that there would be times when you would be put in a compromising position. Like now, for instance. All I can hope for is that you know when you should take an assignment and when you should turn it down." Danny put his arm around me and pulled me close to him.

"I love you too, Danny. I love Carla and the twins, Annie and Mom dearly. I've known for some time that you didn't really like my job. The reason why I took the job as reporter was because I love the excitement of reporting and seeing things in my job. Right now, I'm not sure of the trouble that's going on in Henderson. It may be nothing but rumors. I don't know too much about it. I wonder if I owe it to myself to find out. Besides, I don't want you to worry too much about me. Your black hair will turn white." I then kissed Danny on his cheek and lifted Annie up into my lap. There was nothing that meant more to me than my family.

The party was over and it was time for me to go back home. I had a lot of thinking to do the next two days, and no one could make up my mind but me.

I put baby Annie down and told everyone that it was time for me to leave. They walked me to my car and waved as I drove away.

8

MAKING A DECISION

The next two days were spent walking along the ocean, running through the sand and looking for sea shells. There were times when I would look into the water and hope that someone would look back at me and tell me what I should do.

In no time at all, Monday morning was here and it was time to go to work and give Frank my answer. When I left the house, I walked down to the beach. As I gazed out at the ocean, I imagined myself standing on a small island in the Pacific Ocean, waiting for the tide to come in and carry me far away from land. There was one thing that I had a lot of. A really good imagination!

Once more I stopped daydreaming and walked back up the beach. I could feel the sand rubbing between my toes. As I stood at my car, wiping off my feet, I realized what I had to do. It was time for me to grow up and put the past behind me. By now, everyone had gotten on with a new life.

I got into my car and left for the office. It was much earlier than usual for me to go to work. My usual route was the Santa Monica Boulevard. Today I wanted to avoid the usual traffic jams, so I made a right turn onto Parker Avenue. Then I followed it until I came to the Ridgewood Building. I parked my car in the underground parking lot and then walked past the security guard.

As I entered the building, I looked around to see if I could spot Frank. I said good morning to everyone I passed. Then I walked over to Miss Jones' desk. She was Frank's secretary.

"Miss Jones, will you please tell Mr. Cooper that I'm here? I need to see him as soon as possible. I have a very important matter to discuss with him."

"Right away, Miss Baker. I'll tell him as soon as he comes in." Miss Jones took the papers she had been typing and neatly put them together. Then she tapped them on her desk softly, so that they were stacked in a single pile. She was very efficient and very good at her job. She knew everything about the paper and everyone who worked for it.

I thanked her and walked to the elevator. I pushed the number four button. My office was on the fourth floor. It stopped and I got off. I waved a good morning hello to all of my workers, and then went over to talk with Alice. Alice was my secretary.

"Good morning, Alice. When Mr. Cooper gets here, please send him in right away."

Alice nodded her head and I walked into my office. Before I could put my things away in my drawer and sit down at my desk, Jim Peterson knocked on my office door. Then he walked in. Jim was a tall, good-looking man with blond hair, blue eyes and a wonderful, caring smile and personality. He was the kind of man like the ones you see standing in a store window with a suit on, and as you stand there gazing at the suit, you can't help but notice how gorgeous and well built the man is behind the suit. So you say to yourself, "Man, if only that mannequin was real!" Then out of disappointment, you walk away, feeling cheated for some reason.

"Sarah, how was your weekend?" Jim said as he tilted his head. He could see that I was daydreaming and staring at him with a big, stupid-looking smile on my face. "How was your birthday? Did you drive up the coast to Santa Barbara to see your family?"

"My weekend was wonderful, Jim. They had a nice party for me." Then I looked out at the city. For a split second, I wondered if I had made the right decision.

"Sarah, Frank has asked me to accompany you to Henderson. It looks like we are partners again. I'm sure that Frank told you the rumors about ghosts." Jim laughed aloud and said, "I don't believe in apparitions. There is something going on there, though. We might find ourselves in the middle of a dangerous situation." Jim lit his pipe and walked to the window.

"It might be fun seeing ghosts, Jim!" I laughed back at him. I went to my desk and sat down. "There is someone out there that doesn't want the mine to reopen. Something like this could hurt the town. It took me the entire weekend to decide whether or not I should take the assignment. I'm glad that Frank picked you to go with me to Henderson. When I see him, I will give him my answer. I'm not sure exactly what we will find there. Whatever it might be, I know that we can handle it together."

Jim smiled at me and walked to the door. "Sarah, I would like to take you to dinner tonight to celebrate your birthday."

"You are a little late, but I would love to go with you. Thanks for asking. I'll see you later." As he walked away, my heart felt like it was going a mile a minute. I had waited a long time for Jim to notice me as a woman and not just his newspaper partner.

Frank stuck his head through the doorway to make sure I was there. "Sarah, I heard that you were back and that you wanted to see me right away. Before you give me your answer, please hear me out. I know that I am asking an awful lot of you. If you have any doubts about going back to Henderson, I will understand.

There will be no hard feelings," Frank said as he walked across the room and sat down on the corner of my desk.

"Frank, I'm glad that you are here. I want you to know that I thought long and hard about taking this assignment. I have decided to go to Henderson. I am positive that Jim and I will come across danger while we are there. Someone out there doesn't mind jeopardizing the lives and the jobs of the people of the town."

"You're right. There is something going on there that we aren't sure about yet. I know that there is a story in Henderson. I have every confidence that you and Jim can find it. Tomorrow I will be at the airport to see you both off."

Frank shook my hand and said something cute, like "I'm proud of you, soldier." This was his way of saying thank you for doing this for him. He then turned and walked out of my office.

9

NIGHT CLUB

Before my work was done for the day, I found myself working through lunch and meeting with my camera crew. Before I knew it, the time had passed by very quickly. It was seven o'clock. I was ready to go home.

When I left my office, I went to my secretary's desk and gave her papers that I was sure she would need during the duration I would be away from L.A. and the newspaper. I raised my hand once more to wave goodbye to my fellow coolie. Then I walked away and out the door.

My drive home was beautiful. There is nothing more lovely than the ravishing lights of the city. They sparkled and shone bright like lights hanging from a Christmas tree. I knew that I would miss it dearly while I was away.

When I returned to my home, I went upstairs to the bedroom. I went to my closet and looked thoroughly through my wardrobe. I wanted to dress in an alluring but conservative manner. I was attracted to Jim more than any man I had ever known before. I wanted him to notice me, but I didn't want to give him the wrong message either.

I took a hot bubble bath and finished getting ready for my date.

As I was putting on my necklace, I heard Jim knocking at my front door. I went downstairs and walked to the door to meet him. I handed him my necklace and asked, "Jim, would you hook this latch for me? I always have trouble with it," I said.

"Yes, Sarah. I would love to put my hands around your gorgeous neck. I want this night to be very special for you. Whatever you want to do, or wherever you want to go, is all right with me," Jim said as he latched my necklace.

I smiled at him and said, "Thanks, Jim. I have been looking forward to this evening all day. All I want to do tonight is to be a part of the city and enjoy just being with you for a night full of fun and leisure," I said as we walked to his car.

"One thing I know for sure, there won't be a star in the sky that will ever be as pretty as you are. I can't wait to show you off," Jim said as he held my hand.

Jim's flattery was really making me feel special. I wasn't sure if I would be ready for the evening to end.

We dined and danced the night away at one of the very best restaurants in L.A. Jim asked me to dance and we walked out to the dance floor. I felt as if we were walking on a soft white cloud, with gentle music playing in our ears.

As Jim held me close to him, he looked deeply into my eyes and said, "You are so beautiful, Sarah. Your black hair shines, your blue eyes twinkle like the stars in the sky. Your skin is softer than anything that I have ever touched. The time that we spend in Henderson will give us a chance to be together. This is the opportunity that we need to get to know each other better." At that moment he kissed me for the first time. I put my head on his shoulder, and at that instant I felt very secure and protected.

During the years that we had worked side by side, neither one of us really knew what our real feelings were for one another. In the next few weeks, we could explore the depth of our true feelings. Maybe the time was finally right for us to fall in love. What we didn't know was that the weeks to come would change our lives forever.

When the band stopped playing and the lights were getting dimmer, we left the restaurant and drove back to my home. Jim walked me to my door and put his hand under my chin. He then lifted my head to meet his eyes and he kissed me once again, tenderly on the lips. I felt like I was Cinderella, and my Prince had followed me home from the ball.

"I'll pick you up later, Sarah. We can drive to the airport in my car."

"Okay, Jim, I'll be waiting for tomorrow and your return," I said. What I really wanted to tell him was that I would be counting the minutes and the seconds until I could see him again. That night had been one night that I would hold deep within my heart for the rest of my life.

I went upstairs to bed, where I found myself tossing and turning most of the night until I drifted off to sleep. After a few short hours, my alarm clock sounded loudly, to let me know that it was a new day. I crawled out of bed and got into the shower. As I was bathing, the thoughts of my night with Jim came fluttering back to me. As I got ready for him to pick me up, I couldn't keep my mind on everything that needed to be completed before I could leave

When I finished, I walked down the stairs and I saw Jim coming up my walkway. I met him at the door. I was all packed and ready to go to Henderson, Colorado.

I opened the door and Jim said, "Let me help you with your bags, Sarah. I talked to Frank and he is meeting us at the airport. He has a few things that he wants to discuss with us before we leave L.A." Jim picked up my bags and we walked to his car.

When we arrived at the airport, Frank was standing there, waiting for us. "I won't keep you both for long. I know you have to catch your plane. I just want to tell you that at any time you feel that you need to get out of Henderson, I don't want you to hesitate. Apparently, some of the authorities have found some of the other reporters dead. Some they can't find at all. Be careful, and call me periodically, so that I will know that you are all right." Frank looked worried. He hugged me and shook Jim's hand.

We left for the plane and I could see that even Frank was having second thoughts about whether or not we were doing the right thing.

From L.A. to Denver, Jim and I did a lot of talking. He told me about different jobs that he'd had before he started to work for the *Ridgewood Times* newspaper. I talked to him about the same thing. The flight didn't take long, and before we knew it, the plane was touching down in Denver, Colorado.

The first place we went to was the car rental. Frank had a car waiting for us. All we had to do was sign for it. It was time to go to Henderson.

The drive on the highway through the mountains was wonderful, and the air smelled clean and fresh. The sky was a shade of powder blue.

Henderson was a few hours away from Denver. It had been years since I had been back there to visit. I always managed to stay busy most of my life. I hardly ever allowed myself time out for a vacation.

When we got closer to the town, the different lights seemed to stand out like thousands of twinkle lights reflecting off the mountainside.

We slowed down and turned off an old country road that went past my parents' house. It wasn't far from the highway. When we reached the house, I stopped the car and got out to look at the old homestead. When I was a young girl, I would stand in front of it and make believe that I was a fairy princess who lived in a big castle. Back then, the house looked big to me. I sighed a deep breath. It felt good to be back home once again.

I turned around and went back to the car. Jim was sleeping. I shook him lightly and said, "Jim, wake up. We are here at the house. After we take everything inside, we can go into town and eat."

"That was a short trip," Jim said as he picked up his Western hat off the front car seat. He had bought the hat for our trip to Colorado. He then placed it on his head. He said, "Now I'll fit right in. I'm a real cowboy."

I looked at him and smiled. Then I said, "Jim, it will take more than a Western hat to make you a true cowboy. We'll see how well you do when you ride a horse."

"Speaking of horses, your luggage feels like you packed one for the trip here," Jim said jokingly. "Are we going to take the horses into town, little lady?"

10

MEMORIES AND QUESTIONS

"I don't think we better, Jim. I don't know if the ambulance comes out this far at night," I said.

I unlocked the front door and we took everything inside. Everything was in its rightful place inside the house. No one had changed anything while we were away. Jim and I took covers off of the furniture and then we left for town.

When we got close to town, we saw a small diner. The lights on it were flashing PETE'S DINER. This place was new. We decided that this was the place to stop at.

When we walked through the front door, everyone inside turned their heads to look at us. No one was smiling or talking. They watched us as we walked through the place to a small table in the middle of the room. Suddenly, we felt a chill in the air. We could see that the people there at the diner were not friendly. They would rather see us leave the place. Instead, we stayed.

The waitress came over to our table and asked, "What would you like me to bring you?"

I looked at her and wanted to say, "Nicer people." Instead I said, "We'll look at the menu and decide from it what we want to eat."

I asked Jim, "What do you think? Does this place remind you of a funeral or what?"

"Yes, it does, Sarah. In fact, I have to tell you, I have seen happier faces on people at a funeral home than this place."

Soon the waitress returned to get our order. We told her what we wanted and watched her walk over to talk to the cook. They kept looking over at us. Jim and I knew that there was something strange about that place. Everyone in there was watching us.

After we finished eating, I excused myself from the table and went to the ladies' room. As I stood there washing my hands, I happened to look down at the floor. Lying on the floor was a piece of paper that hadn't been there when I entered the room. I bent down to pick it up. I was getting ready to put it into the waste basket when I saw the message that was on it. The paper read:

GET OUT OF HERE! LEAVE AND GO HOME!

I left the room as quickly as I could and went back to the table and Jim. I handed him the note. I said to him, "Did you see anyone standing over by the door? Someone slid this note under it. I'm not sure if it is meant for us."

"Sarah, we haven't even been here a day and trouble is already finding us. Look around the room and see if there is anyone in here that you might know from the past."

I looked around at all the people. There was no one in the room that I recognized.

"No, Jim. I don't know anyone in here. Whoever it was must have gone out a different door."

We got up from the table and walked to the door to leave. When we were outside, I told Jim that it was like a breath of fresh air to be out of that place. He agreed with me. That was one place that we had vowed never to go back to.

When we were driving back to the house, we saw something up ahead of us in the road. Jim slowed down and put his lights on bright. Then I heard him yell, "What the hell is that?"

We were approaching something that appeared to be an object of some sort. As we got closer, we could see that the object wasn't an object at all. It was a small child sitting in the middle of the road, eating a dead animal that had been struck by a car. The child was a girl. As we passed her, she jumped toward our car.

"Hurry, Sarah, roll the window up!" Jim screamed. "Something isn't right with her. I can't believe my eyes. What could possibly make that girl eat a dead animal from the road?" Jim said as he swerved away from the child. Jim drove faster until we were back at the house.

After we stopped the car in front, I said, "I don't know what to say, Jim. Frank is right. Things have changed around here. Something bad is happening and I feel like we are right in the midst of it."

There was nothing more to say. Jim went to bed and I went outside to sit on the old porch swing. I could feel the stillness of the night. I had forgotten how beautiful the town of Henderson was. There were so many memories that I had stored inside of me. I could see my dad working on our old Buick. Mom was standing at her clothesline, hanging up the clothes that she had spent hours washing. My brother, Danny, was climbing up the ladder of his tree house. All of the memories that I had in my head seemed like yesterday. I knew that it was time to put them to rest! Things could never be the same again.

Jim and I had a story to do for the newspaper. I had to find out who the person was that slid the note under the door at the diner tonight, and why. Someone wanted Jim and me to leave here pretty badly! The question that kept going through my mind was why? It was going to take both of us to solve this mystery!

I stood up. It was time to go back in the house.

Hopefully, things would be brighter tomorrow.

The following morning, Jim found me out by the corral. I had gotten a saddle out of the shed and was in the process of putting it on one of the horses. The horses that we kept belonged to my Aunt Carol She is my dad's sister.

Jim put a saddle on a horse and climbed on. He then said, "Which end do I sit on first?" He laughed as he faced the horse backwards. He clowned around for a while. Then he turned around and rode off, doing tricks that I had only seen at the rodeo. I felt silly for teasing him about riding a horse. He was truly the best horseman that I had ever seen.

"Jim, where did you ever learn to ride like that? I know, while on the plane, we discussed our past before we both moved to L.A. You never fail to amaze me!"

Jim climbed off of his horse and replied, "There's a lot that you don't know about me. I grew up on a ranch in Texas. I know that I don't have an accent. I lost it before I met you. I also come from a small town. I rode bulls in the rodeo during the time when I was growing up. You might say that a horse is a big part of me. I wasn't trying to fool you. Sarah. I only wanted to see your smile and hear your laughter. Don't blame yourself for something that you didn't know about."

Once again, Jim held my face in his hands. I could tell that he was going to kiss me. His grip was strong and firm. Yet his hands were soft and gentle. For the first time in my life, I was feeling passion. I felt safe, and most of all I knew that he would always be there for me, to protect me from whatever might occur while we were in Henderson.

We climbed onto the horses and rode down the country road in the direction of the mine. Jim held onto his hat so that the gusts of wind blowing in his face wouldn't whip it off of his head. He looked so cute in it. At times, he would turn to me and smile. I would smile back at him. We rode side by side. Occasionally, we would hold hands. Once or twice, he would lean over toward me and look into my eyes. Then he would steal a kiss or two.

As our horses galloped away together, we could feel the warm air against our skin. When he looked into my eyes, I knew that I was falling in love. I was sure that he, too, felt the same way.

When we were riding past Casey and Betty Smith's house, Betty saw us. She recognized me. The last time that we had seen each other was when I was 16. She waved and motioned for me to come over to her.

"Sarah Baker, how are you? It's good to see you again. What have you been doing with yourself all these years?" she asked.

I climbed off my horse and walked over to her. "It's wonderful seeing you again, Betty. I have been living in Santa Monica, California. This is my partner, Jim Peterson." At that time, Jim tilted his hat at her in a gesture of saying hello. "We work for the *Ridgewood Times* newspaper. We both are reporters. The company that bought the old Henderson Mine invited us here to do a story on the reopening ceremony."

"Sarah, it sounds to me like you and your friend are not aware of what's going on now in Henderson. You shouldn't have come back here!" Betty's expression changed. Before, she had looked very happy to see me. Now her face was full of fear.

"What is it, Betty, that we should know about? Tell us what it is that we are supposed to be afraid of. Before we left L.A., we were told of unusual happenings. Some of the rumors I don't want to believe," I told Betty as I squeezed her hand.

"I don't know what rumors you heard about, Sarah. If it's what I think it is, they are true. The town held a meeting last week. Everyone was forced to attend. We were warned not to talk to a stranger, or give out any information about the old Henderson Mine or the town. I wish I could talk you into leaving this place right away. If you decide to stay, be careful, Sarah. They will be watching every move that you make." At that time, Betty squeezed my hand as I had hers. She wanted to show me that she was concerned about our safety and what could happen to us.

"I'm sorry, Betty. Jim and I just got here. There is no way that we can leave Henderson now. Today we are going to take pictures of the workers and the mine."

"The workers there won't let you take pictures, Sarah. Different parts of the mine are still boarded up. Stay away from it. When you go into town, be careful! Not everyone who lives here now is friendly. Watch your back, Sarah. Don't trust anyone."

I walked away from her and climbed back onto my horse. "Once again, Betty, I'm sorry. I wish that we could do what you want us to do. Don't worry. We will be careful."

I could tell by the look on her face that she was terrified of something or someone. I waved to her and Jim and I rode away. When I turned around to look back at her, she looked very sad and worried. She looked as if she would never see us again alive.

Fifteen years ago, Betty got real sick. She had to go to the hospital. It was during the time when Casey needed to get his crops in. Since Casey and Betty didn't have much money, my dad helped them out. This way, Casey could be with her. Mom and I took care of their children.

When Fred Anderson's barn caught on fire, everyone in the valley got together and helped him. Before, everyone was more than happy to help each other in their time of need.

As Jim and I got closer to the mine, the air smelled sour. It seemed to stand still. We climbed off of our horses and tied them up. We walked up the hill toward the mine. Everything around the area was dead. There was a time when the hillside was covered with green grass, green trees and wildflowers. Now there was nothing there but dirt.

The old Indians that live around Henderson have a saying that goes like this: "Anyone that dares walk on stolen land will curse the day until he should die!" The land that the mine was on had once belonged to the Indians, until the white man took it away from them. Somehow the Indians could never forgive them for it. From the looks of things, it really did look like a curse had been put on the land. The company had put signs up, telling people to keep out of the mine. The area that surrounded the mine looked like an old cemetery that no one wanted to take care of anymore.

There were a lot of men working there today. The company that bought the mine was busy getting it ready for the reopening. There was a young man on a dozer that had noticed us standing there. He climbed down and went over to talk to an older man who was wearing a suit. The man looked like he might be one of the bosses. Now they were both looking up here at us. The man in the suit was leaving in a Jeep, and the young man was going back to work with his dozer. There were several workers there today. Betty must be wrong about them not wanting us here, taking pictures. No one had come up here to tell us to leave.

Jim got a lot of good pictures for the newspaper. We started walking down the hill to leave. I happened to look ahead at Jackson Mountain. To my disbelief, I saw something that was different than anything I had ever seen before. There were odd-looking people standing there, watching everything that we did. These people were pale-complected with eyes that were tinted red, like the flames from a forest fire. I wanted to take a picture of them, but something told me not to. Maybe I had seen what the passing tourists believed to be ghosts. Somehow there had to be a logical explanation for everything that had been happening around here!

"Jim, I'm really glad that you came with me to Henderson. I came up here, thinking that I would still see the land and the mine the way it was before. I can't believe how much all of it has changed. I just now saw some strange-looking people standing on Jackson Mountain, watching us. I am sure that they noticed that I saw them, too. I feel like they can see right through us."

"Don't worry, Sarah. I took pictures of the mountain. If there is anything to be alarmed about, it will show up on a picture," Jim said as he untied our horses.

Maybe what he had said was supposed to make me feel better, but it didn't. What I had seen was very real. If I didn't believe in a walking corpse before, I did now!

11

AN AGREEMENT
TO HELP

We rode back to the house without stopping to talk to anyone. Jim put the horses in the corral. I went inside to get the film in the camera ready for processing.

In the old house there was a large closet that was located in one of the bedrooms. We were going to use the closet for the developing.

By subjecting the exposed photographic film to the developer, I was able to bring the picture into view. When Jim came into the closet, he took the pictures out of the developer and held them very carefully. Then he said, "I'll be damned! Sarah, you were right! Take a good look at what showed up in a picture. By the looks of this, I don't blame you for being afraid! These people have the same characteristics as the small girl that was sitting in the middle of the road. Somehow I feel like it's Halloween all over again. These people look like ghouls. I can't wait to send these pictures to Frank. He won't believe what he's about to see!" Jim said with great intensity.

"We really should go back there, Jim, and try to talk to those people. There is definitely something weird going on around Henderson! Let's go back into town. Maybe we can find someone that will explain all of this to us."

"I agree. I'm ready whenever you are."

Jim took the pictures to the dresser. Then he put them in the top drawer. We went back downstairs and left the house.

On our way to Henderson, we decided that it would be better, after we entered town, to go in separate directions. This would give us the opportunity to talk to different people. By doing this, we could cover more ground.

While driving down the streets, we still found ourselves to be a big attraction. People were staring at us as if we were freaks from a side show that had come to town with the circus.

I got out of the car on Main Street. I crossed the street and walked down the old cracked sidewalk, looking in all the store windows. I was headed for the drugstore. There was one person in Henderson that I knew that I could trust. He had always been a friend of my family. I was fairly sure that he would still remember me.

I stopped at the window of his store and looked in. Then I opened the door and went in. The drugstore hadn't changed much. The old soda fountain was still there. I sat down on one of the stools as I had from years that had gone by. Soon a clerk approached me.

"Yes, can I be of help to you?" the clerk asked.

"Yes, you can. Can you tell me if Mr. Walker is still here?" I said.

"Indeed he is. Let me get him for you." The clerk left and went into the storage room in the back of the store. I sat on the old stool, waiting. Soon I saw Mr. Walker poke his bald head out to look around the room. He wanted to know who it was that had wanted to talk to him. When he saw me, he said, "Sarah Baker, you are still as pretty as early morning snow! It has been a lot of years since I have seen you. I heard that you and your family moved to Los Angeles after the mine shut down. How are your folks? Did you hear about the new company from the East buying the mine?"

"Yes, Mr. Walker, it's been a long time. It's good seeing you also! I did hear that a company from back East bought the mine. That is the reason why I came back here. I work for a newspaper in L.A. called the *Ridgewood Times*. My partner and I were sent here to do a story on it. My mom is fine, Mr. Walker. My dad was found dead about six months ago. No one could find out why he died," I said.

I paused for a few seconds to clear my throat, and then I said, "I have a reason for coming to see you today. When my partner Jim and I arrived here, strange things started happening to us. Nobody here will tell us what's going on now in Henderson. I knew that if there was anybody here that I could count on for help, it would be you."

"I'm real sorry to hear about your dad, Sarah. He was a good man and a kind person to everyone. I'm happy your mom is okay. I want you to know that it's not that I don't want to help you. You picked a bad time to come back to Henderson. Everyone who lives here has been threatened to keep their mouths shut. We have been warned about talking to anyone about what is going on here. I am sure that you won't find a soul that will help you." Mr. Walker then turned his head in several directions, to look around the room. He was very fidgety and wanted to make sure that no one was watching us.

"Mr. Walker, I can understand why you feel that you should keep still. I'm sorry that someone is threatening everyone in town. Whether you or anyone else chooses to help us is up to you. Whatever you decide won't make a difference. My partner and I won't go anywhere until we get what we came after. I thought maybe you would help us and tell me what is out there, and what it is that we are up against. We won't know how to stop them without your help. I guess I was wrong in coming to you."

I had said what I came there to say. I couldn't make him tell me anything. I turned to walk away when Mr. Walker grabbed my elbow. He said, "All right, Sarah. You always did have a special place in my heart. I will help you and your friend. I will tell you what you need to know. I can't tell you here. There are too many ears that might overhear us talking. I don't want to put you, myself, or my family in danger. I'll meet you at your parents' old house later on tonight."

Mr. Walker then walked away. It was time for me to leave and find Jim. I couldn't wait to tell him that finally I had found someone willing to help us.

I left the drugstore and was walking down the sidewalk when I saw Jim standing across the street in front of the town market. He was talking to a man. By the time I could get over to them, the man had left Jim standing there all alone. The man had gone back inside the store.

I told Jim the news and started helping put items that he had bought into the car. I noticed an odd-looking man across the street beside a building. He was watching us. When I looked at him, he ducked behind it as if he didn't want us to see him standing there.

At the time, Jim was bent over inside the back seat of the car. He was putting something on the floor when I said loudly, "Jim!"

It startled him and he said, "What?"

"There's a man over there behind that building. He was watching us." My voice sounded frantic. I was afraid.

It was time to see why we were being watched. "Stay here and I'll see if I can catch up with him." Jim ran over to where I had seen the man standing. It was too late. He had disappeared out of sight.

When we were driving back to the house, Jim told me that he had tried to talk to several people during the time when I was in the drugstore. Mr. Walker was right. Nobody would tell him anything. It was apparent that everyone in town was overcome by a huge amount of fear brought on by someone or something. There was something imminent going on in the town of Henderson. Whatever it was, I knew that it had to be bigger than what we originally thought it to be.

While in town, Jim had bought new locks and latches for the doors and windows. He also bought a gun, which we both hoped we wouldn't have to use.

The night progressed without a trace of Mr. Walker. I watched the old grandfather clock on the wall chime eleven o'clock. It was getting late. He should have been here before now. Mr. Walker was always a man of his word. He wouldn't let me down unless there was a good reason. I was terrified that something bad had happened to him.

"You look tired, Sarah. Why don't you go up to bed? I'll stay down here and wait for Mr. Walker to come," Jim said.

"I know that I can't sleep, Jim. I have been sitting here thinking. I have a feeling that something bad might have happened to him. I was really counting on him for help and for answers." I was worried and concerned about the safety of Mr. Walker.

"Maybe he changed his mind, Sarah. Maybe he thought it to be too dangerous and risky for his family. After we are done with our story, we can leave

Henderson and go back home to L.A. Mr. Walker, on the other hand, can't. He has to live here."

There was nothing more to say. I knew that Jim was right. We waited a little longer. For some unknown reason, I had a gut feeling that he wasn't coming. Where could he be?

The next day Jim and I went into town. I had to make sure that Mr. Walker was still all right. We drove down Main Street and parked the car in front of the drugstore. I noticed that the "YES, WE'RE OPEN" sign was facing the opposite way. It was too late in the day for the store to still be closed.

I looked at Jim and said, "That's strange. The store should be open by now."

We continued to walk up to the door. I tried opening the door knob. When I turned it to go inside, I was stopped by the same clerk that I had talked to the day before.

"Excuse me. I'm the woman that was here yesterday to see Mr. Walker. Can I please see him again today? It's urgent that I speak to him once more," I told the clerk.

"Yes, you can see him. If you don't mind going to the town morgue. Mr. Walker was in an accident last night. I'm closing up the store. That's the way his family wants it."

Suddenly, I was filled with remorse. I stood there, not knowing what to say to the clerk as she shut the door. I had tears running down my face. I couldn't shake the feeling that it was my fault why Mr. Walker was dead. If he wouldn't have been out driving to my house, he would still be alive. I should never have asked him for help.

Jim held me close to him. He could see that I was

without words. "What do you want to do now, Sarah? Do you want to go back to L.A.? If the answer is no, do you know anyone else in town that might help us?"

"Yes, Jim, I do. It's hard for me to ask her, now that this has happened. My Aunt Carol is still alive. I wasn't ready to visit her yet, but now I realize that she might be the only one in Henderson who is willing to help us. Right now, there's one thing that I need to do. There's only one way to know for sure if Mr. Walker is really dead. We need to go to the town morgue."

It wasn't that I didn't believe the clerk exactly. All I knew was that there were a lot of really weird stuff going on, and if I ever felt mixed up and confused, it was today.

"When we get in there, we can hide until it is safe to find out where they are keeping him." This was going to be fun. I wasn't real big on morgues. Anything that ever pertained to death always scared the hell out of me. It might be hard to tell how Mr. Walker died! It was like a force was bound and determined to keep us away from the truth.

Jim laughed at me. Then he said, "Sarah, there is nothing in the morgue that will hurt you. Dead people don't know that they are dead. I'm glad to see that you have your sense of humor back again. It's not your fault why he died. Once again, I feel that it has to do with the morbid town."

We went to the morgue, hoping that no one would see us trying to get in. Once we were in there, hopefully it wouldn't be long before we could get out. It was easier getting in there than I had thought. There was a small coat closet where we stood, patiently waiting for the two men to leave. Then it was time for us to look.

Jim pulled out several drawers that contained

bodies. Finally we found him. I grabbed Jim's arm. What I saw frightened me! "Look at that hole in his neck!" I was scared. It was hard for me to move.

"I'm looking, Sarah! Most of me refuses to believe what I'm seeing. His neck is ripped apart."

"Could a car accident have done this to him? What do you think, Jim?"

"I don't know what to think. I guess a car accident could have done this. Then again, a wild animal could have done it. Let's close the drawer and get out of here. I'll take some quick pictures of Mr. Walker's neck and body."

When Jim had finished taking the pictures for Frank, we pushed the drawer that Mr. Walker's body was lying in back into the wall. We both looked around to make sure that no one had entered the building without us seeing them. We were safe. No one had seen us in there.

This day had been very interesting and frightening. The worst part was that it wasn't over with yet!

12

VISITING AUNT CAROL

Instead of going back to the house, we did the one thing that I didn't want to do. No matter what was taking place in Henderson, I didn't want to involve my Aunt Carol. She was an old woman and I feared for her safety if she helped us in any way.

There was something very mysterious out there in the night that had to be stopped. I didn't know if Jim and I could do it, but we had to try!

So, instead of going back to the house, we went to visit my Aunt Carol. As we drove down her lane, we could see servants standing all around.

Jim stopped the car. We got out and walked up the path that led to her front door. I had forgotten how big her house was.

Once again we found ourselves being stared at. Frankly, it was starting to annoy me. In the words of my brother Danny, "The correct way to handle a situation of this sort is to stick out your tongue or drop the pants and shoot the moon at them. Then they would have something to look at." In my mind I could hear Danny telling me that I guess I was more homesick than I thought I was. I was really trying hard to be an adult about the way the people were treating us. It was getting old and I knew that before long I would probably forget my age and go for it!

I stuck my hand up to knock on the door. Everything felt so strange and spooky to me. Once again, my imagination took over and I felt like Jim and I had stepped out of the present time period that we were in, into the past, and in an Addam's Family movie. I expected to see Lurch greeting us at the door. Instead, an elderly woman answered it.

"May I help you?" asked the woman.

"Yes, I've come to see Carol Baker. I am her niece, Sarah Baker." Before I could say anything else, my aunt entered the room. For some mysterious reason, she was in a wheelchair. It seemed strange to me that she would be in one. Mom never mentioned that she had gotten hurt.

"Sarah, is it really you?" my aunt asked.

"Yes, Aunt Carol. It is really me. This is Jim Peterson. He is my friend and partner from the newspaper in L.A., where we work. We are news reporters."

"Sarah, what are you doing here? You and your friend must leave Henderson and go back to California right away."

"Tell me why, Aunt Carol. Why do we need to leave right away?" It was clear to me that she also knew something that she didn't want to talk about. I was sick of everyone telling us to get out of town, but no one was telling us exactly why or what for!

"I wish I could say, Sarah. All I can tell you is this. Henderson is not the small, friendly town that it was before. It has changed. You aren't safe here! It's too late for me. I can't leave. I want you and your friend to get out while you can."

"We can't leave now, Aunt Carol. We have come back here to do a story for the newspaper that we work for. You say that Henderson has changed. Tell me how it has changed. We need your help. There's no one else that I can trust around here."

"Sarah, there is very little that I can tell you without endangering your life. The less you know about what is going on here, the better off you will be. You have to believe me."

"We won't leave until after the opening of the old Henderson Mine."

"Stay away from the mine, Sarah! They will never let it reopen!"

Jim sat down on the sofa. He looked into Aunt Carol's eyes and said, "Who do you mean by they?"

"I'm sorry. I've said too much as it is!" Those were the last words she muttered about everything that we had asked her to help us with.

I tried several times to get her to talk to me about whatever it was that had Henderson in an uproar. After a while, I realized that she wasn't going to reveal anything to me. All she wanted to do was talk about the way it was in the past, when my family still lived in Henderson before we moved to California.

We had stayed longer than we intended. We had promised Frank that we would call him today with some news for the paper. We told my aunt goodbye and then we left the house.

It was pitch dark outside. There were no stars in the sky. Once more, we had to walk down the path that led from the house to our car. There were willow trees that were up and down the path. It was spooky to walk through there. The willows looked like arms stretched out to grab whomever would dare to enter their surroundings.

When we got to the car, Jim looked at me and said, "You know, Sarah, I would never say or do anything to hurt you. I know that your aunt is old and set in her ways. I must say, though, that there is no excuse for her behavior today. She should have helped you. You are her niece. I feel that she is jerking you around.

Your life could be in danger."

"Jim, I appreciate your honesty. You are entitled to your opinion. Maybe she knew that she was being watched and she didn't want to endanger our lives or hers."

"I can't help feeling that there is more to her and what's going on than she wants us to know. Time will tell!"

As we drove down the lane, we saw lights flashing on the highway. When we got closer to the lights, Jim steered the car off to the side of the road. It looked as if a car was on fire.

A man came over to our car and told us that we could continue with caution. As we got closer to the car, we got a good look at it. It was exactly like the one that we were driving. We both felt that either that was one big coincidence, or someone was trying to kill us!

When we drove up to the house, we saw that there was a flare on the mailbox. Jim stopped the car and walked back to it. Inside was another note which read: GO HOME! YOU ARE NOT WELCOME HERE! GET OUT WHILE YOU CAN! There was no turning back now! It was time to find out who was sending us the notes.

In the morning I was awakened by the sound of a large truck coming from the direction of the old Henderson Mine.

I heard Jim go down the stairs. Then I heard the front door close. He had gone outside to look at something.

I put my bathrobe on and left my room. I also went downstairs and outside. I wanted to see what it was that Jim was looking at.

It had rained last night. The ground was soft and

we could see something that resembled footprints. While I was lying in my bed during the night, I could hear the horses in the corral. They were very restless. I thought maybe a storm was coming, or a bobcat might be close by. Whatever the footprints came from had the horses terrified. They appeared to be long and narrow. They were different than any that I had ever seen, and didn't look like prints from an animal.

When my family lived here, we had heard rumors about Bigfoot sightings in the area. I was sure that the footprints we had found today weren't from anything so bizarre as that.

"Sarah, I think it's time for us to talk to the sheriff," Jim said. "From the looks of these footprints, there is something out there that is stalking this area. Maybe he will give us some answers on a lot of strange things we've seen since we arrived here."

"Maybe you're right, Jim. There are a lot of really weird things that have been happening since we came here. Whatever it is that these footprints came from could be very dangerous. Last night, when I heard the horses out here running back and forth around the corral, I got up out of bed and looked out my window. It was so dark, I couldn't see anything, but I could tell that the horses were frantic. The wind was blowing hard and there were a lot of gusts. I thought maybe there was a storm on its way. I can see today that I was wrong. There has to be a logical reason for all of this," I said to Jim.

I went back into the house and got ready to go to town. Then we left.

We went straight to the sheriff's office. We opened the door and went in. There at the desk was the sheriff. He was an older man. He looked like he was about the same age as my parents.

We walked over to him and I said, "Excuse me. I'm Sarah Baker and this is Jim Peterson. We are newspaper reporters from L.A. that have come back here to do a story on the old Henderson Mine. Since we arrived, there have been a lot of strange things that have been happening to us. Our first night, we saw a small girl sitting in the middle of the road, eating a dead animal. She lunged at the car. We were given a couple of notes threatening us if we didn't leave Henderson. Last night, someone or something was stalking the grounds around the corral. We found odd-looking footprints today. We've asked several people to help us out by telling us what's going on in this town. No one wants to help. We thought maybe we should come here and talk to you about it. Can you help us?" I asked.

"Well, young lady, I am sure that whatever it is that you think is going on isn't! The notes might be coming from some children in the neighborhood. After all, some people just plain don't like city folk. Has anyone tried to harm you physically? If the answer is no, I suggest that you go back to the city before it's too late."

Jim told the sheriff that we weren't going anywhere until we had the story for the newspaper. Once again, we had come up with nothing. As my dad would have said, "The well has run dry." It was plain to see that the sheriff didn't like us and wasn't going to be obliging.

We felt as if the trip into town was a waste of our time. Maybe if we drove out to the mine, we could find the people from Jackson Mountain and ask them questions.

We left town and drove out there. Jim parked the

car below the hill. We walked up the hill, hoping to see the people. There was no one in sight for us to talk to.

"I don't see those people, Jim. I know a way down into the mine. Let's go down there and look around. Maybe there is a clue there that we can find. I can see that the portal is still closed off. If we want to go down there, we will have to go through an opening that not too many people know about. It's close by. Follow me."

After searching, I found the opening. Jim crawled through it first. Then I went through. We walked around down there for several hours. We shone a flashlight in different directions. There didn't seem to be anyone else down there. We were ready to leave the mine and go back up on top when we heard noises coming from up ahead.

Not knowing what or who it was, Jim said, "Sarah, turn off the flashlight. Get down on the ground. We don't know who is making that noise. If it's a person, we can't trust him yet. Let's crawl a little closer, so we can find out what the noise is."

I did what Jim had said. Up ahead was the sheriff. We had just talked to him in town. We were surprised to see him in the mine. He was standing there, talking to some men.

"I thought I told you to get rid of those city kids! Before long we will have more newspaper people here, snooping around and interfering with the way things are around here! They came into my office today wanting answers!"

Finally, the truth was starting to come out! Now we knew the reason why no one wanted us here. They were afraid of us because we were newspaper people. There was a secret that the sheriff and the people of Henderson didn't want us to find out! Whatever it was must be awfully big.

"We're sorry, sheriff. We tried to get rid of them. We set fire to a car that we thought was theirs. Turned out it belong to old man Jenson. Boy, was he madder than a wet hen!"

The sheriff and his men walked away, talking, and soon they were out of sight and hearing distance. Jim and I stayed in place and remained quiet until we knew for sure that they weren't coming back and that we were safe.

"Sarah, we have to get out of here now! I guess going to see the sheriff wasn't such a bad idea after all. We are starting to find out what the townspeople don't want us to know about. Let's go back into town and wait for the sheriff to return to his office. If we follow him, maybe he will lead us to finding the key to this mystery."

We crawled on the floor of the mine for a while, and then we got up and walked back to the opening that we had come through. It seemed that danger had found us and we weren't ready for it.

13

REVEALING INFORMATION

After we were out of the mine, we went back to town. I felt a cold chill in the air. The streets were empty and it appeared that the town of Henderson was experiencing a blackout. Henderson looked like a ghost town!

Jim parked our car in an alley off a side street. From there, we walked down the alley to the main street. Then we went to the sheriff's office. Jim was right. He had come back into town. He was sitting at his desk with candles lit. Jim crouched down to look through a corner of the window. I stood behind him, watching every move in the night. I could see shadows from the trees and the bushes, but so far no one was in sight! I continued to watch the street as Jim watched the sheriff. He was talking on the phone. After a while, he got up from his desk and put his hat on. He then went out the back door of his office.

We went around to the alley and followed him. He went into Mr. Walker's drugstore through a spare room that was facing the alley.

Jim and I went around front and watched the sheriff through a crack in the door. He was standing there, watching his men bring wooden boxes out of the storage room. They appeared to be crates that Mr. Walker had used to store contents in his store. The men were taking them out the back door and putting them in a big truck that had entered the alley behind the store. The truck looked to be the same one I had seen coming down the road outside my bedroom window early in the morning.

After the truck was loaded, the sheriff and his men climbed in the back and it left. Jim and I were sure that it was on its way back to the mine. We knew that it would be better if we waited until morning to do anything else. There wasn't a way that we could get back down into the mine to see where they were unloading the truck before it would leave the area.

We were driving back to the house, and I noticed how quiet Jim was. I could tell that he was thinking about something. When we reached the house, he looked at me and said, "Sarah, the sheriff was right. I'm starting to realize what it is that everyone is so afraid of. The first thing that we noticed about the people of Henderson was their fear and unfriendliness. Then we saw that small girl in the road, eating the meat and blood of a dead animal! You saw those weird-looking people up by Jackson Mountain that looked like the walking dead! Then we saw the sheriff and his men loading wooden crates on the truck. They had to be taking them down into a dark place. We know this place is the mine! We found Mr. Walker with his neck half eaten and a piercing hole in it. There is only one explanation for all of this. Some of the people in Henderson are without a doubt Nosferatu!"

Everything that Jim had told me made sense. I never thought that those creatures existed until now. They have also been referred to as ghouls or creatures of the night. That is the way to explain the people from Jackson Mountain. There was nothing human about them. What Jim had told me scared the hell out of me. If this was true, we were going to fight for our lives. Now, more than ever, we had to go back to my aunt's house. There had to be a way that we could protect ourselves. Aunt Carol knew what it is, and this time we would find a way to make her tell us what she knew.

We were sure now that the only ones we could trust would be each other. What we found in Henderson was more than a story for the newspaper. It was becoming personal.

We went into the house. There, Jim poured himself a drink and lit his pipe. He sat down on the sofa beside me. We both knew that it wouldn't be long before the evil beings that had taken over the small town would be coming to harm and kill us. Each night had gotten longer and the days seemed to get shorter.

Jim got up from his chair and went into the kitchen. I also got up and went over to the window. It was hard for me to understand why this had to happen to my hometown. The night looked so peaceful and quiet. It was hard to believe that there was something out there somewhere that would attack innocent people in their sleep.

My mom and dad didn't take everything with them when we left here. I knew that my dad had left behind a lot of his old books. There was one thing that I was sure that he hadn't meant to leave behind. It was his journal. I stood there, turning pages and laughing at different ideas that he had written about, when I came to a paragraph that had been entered before the mine caught on fire and was shut down.

It read: "Today is not like any other. I have come across something that I am afraid to tell anyone about. When I went to work, I found evil down in the mine that I can't explain. The town is going to change now that this has happened. There is no way that it will ever be the same. MAY GOD HELP US ALL!"

I stood there, staring at what I had just read. I

thumbed through the journal, looking for more. There was none. Whatever it was that my dad was writing about had scared him more than anyone could imagine.

After Jim came back into the room, I showed him the page. While we were looking through the journal, we heard a noise coming from the study.

"Sarah, stay here. I'll go see what it is."

I watched Jim as he silently opened up the swinging door. He left the light out and crept into the room. There was no one there. He went to the window to look outside. Out on the patio he saw a beautiful young woman standing there, smiling at him. Her white dress that she was wearing was pressed tightly against her tall, sleek body, and it flowed softly in the wind. Her hair shone brighter than the sun when the moon lit up the sky. She stood there, motioning for him to join her outside. She would smile and dance around the flower garden, swaying from side to side, in hopes of enticing him into opening the door and going out into the night air. Jim kept watching the young woman and her every move. She had him in a trance.

I waited for him to come back. When he didn't, I got worried and went to the study to find him. When I entered the room, I could see the young woman and the way that she had Jim under her spell! I turned on the light in hopes of bringing him out of it.

At that instant, I could see the young woman change from a beautiful woman into an old hag right before my eyes! Her face turned old and ugly. She hissed and scowled at me. She reared her ugly head back and showed me her fangs. The bony fingers on her wrinkled hands lunged out at me! She was very angry. Then she ran away into the night.

I called Jim's name several times and he continued

to stare out the window. He wasn't hearing anything I said to him. I walked over to him and shook him until he responded to me. He had a dazed expression on his face. I knew that what I had seen on the patio wasn't human. The Nosferatu were going to make sure that we knew that they were out there. Now we knew that we would have to kill them before they killed us!

As we walked back into the living room, the house shook. The window rattled and the pictures that were on the wall tilted to one side. The furniture fell over and the lamp that was on the table by the couch tipped over and hit the floor.

Jim and I had made the evil creature of the night angry. We both knew that we hadn't seen the last of them!

The next day, while driving back to Aunt Carol's house, we stopped to talk to Casey and Betty Smith. Casey was outside, working on his tractor, and Betty was at her garden, pulling weeds. When we drove up to their house, they saw us and came over to our car to speak with us.

"Sarah Baker, you are a sight for sore eyes! It's been too long since we've seen you! Betty told me that you and your friend had stopped by here the other day. What brings you back out this way?" It had been a long time since I had heard Casey's voice. It was good to see that he hadn't lost his Irish manner after all these years.

"It's been quite a while, Casey. You haven't changed much. We are on our way to my aunt's house. I have something that I would like you to take a look at. It concerns my dad. Last night I was looking through my parents' things when I came across Dad's old journal. It's the one that he had the last year that the old Henderson Mine was open, before the fire and explosion. I know that you both were good friends. Did he say something to you about what he saw in the mine that scared him?" I asked Casey.

I opened the journal to the page that I wanted Casey to read. I watched his face turn white with fear. There was sweat running off of it. He looked at Betty. She had put her hand over her mouth. It was plain for me to see that whatever my dad had written about that night, a long time ago, had come back to haunt Casey and Betty once more.

Casey looked up at me and said, "I wish that I could help you, Sarah. Betty told me that you had asked her several questions when you were here before. Your dad was more than a friend to me. Your family was very good to mine. If I tell you anything, it will put all of our lives in great danger. Right now, you and your friend can leave and go back to California. Our lives are here on this ranch. We have no place that we can run to. Don't spend too much time thinking about what your dad wrote about, Sarah. Back then we all thought we saw things that we really didn't see."

"I do understand your situation, Casey. There is no way that I ever want to bring harm to your family. I only wish that there was something that I could do to help you."

At that point Casey opened his mouth to say something. Instead, Betty spoke. "There is nothing more to say, Sarah. We have a lot of work we need to get back to." After Betty had said that, Casey got back on his tractor and told me that he wished the best for us. Betty said goodbye and we got back into the car.

When we drove away, I knew that Aunt Carol was our only hope of finding out how to stop the fiends that had taken over the town of Henderson and the mine. There was a part of me that was very angry. It looked like the whole town was too weak to fight back.

When we reached Aunt Carol's house, we noticed that Sheriff Connors' car was parked up the road. Casey Smith was wrong about my dad. He would never write anything in his journal that wasn't true! I knew that whatever it was he had seen that night was very real! I was sure that both Casey and Betty knew what that something was that he had written about. They, too, were afraid of whatever it was.

Jim and I got out of the car once again and walked up the path that led to Aunt Carol's front door. This was the day when we had to find a way to make my aunt tell us what she knew.

Raking leaves along the pathway was a gray-haired man. He looked to be one of Aunt Carol's servants. We stopped walking and I tapped him on the shoulder. When he turned around, I said, "I'm sorry to bother you. Can you tell us if Carol Baker is at home?"

The old man didn't hesitate when he said, "Please excuse me, madam. I'm not allowed to speak to you."

With those words, Jim and I continued walking up to the house. Jim was convinced that he had seen my aunt standing at the window, watching us. If she was standing, why would she be trying to make us think that she was confined to a wheelchair?

Jim knocked on the door and a tall, pale-faced, slender man answered. He asked, "Can I be of service to you?"

"Yes, we have come to see Carol Baker."

"Please come in and I will tell her that you are here."

"Thank you," I said to the man.

After we were inside the house, we were taken to Aunt Carol's library. There we were told to sit down and wait for her. The man said that Aunt Carol would join us shortly.

"Sarah, before your aunt gets here, I need to talk to you about something."

"What is it, Jim?" I asked.

"While we were walking up here, I am positive that I not only saw your aunt standing, but I also saw her talking to Sheriff Conners at the windows. I'm not saying that she is mixed up with him. I don't know what to think. I'm going to go see if I can find them and try to overheat whatever it is that they are talking about."

I could tell that he was afraid to leave me alone. He and I both knew that this was the only way to get information that we needed. He got up from where he was sitting and went to the door. He carefully opened it and looked out to see if anyone was watching the room that we were in. Then he walked silently down the hall, listening at every door. He heard nothing. As he was getting ready to come back to the library, he heard Aunt Carol and the sheriff talking outside on the porch. He went closer, so that he could hear what was being said.

"So, you understand, Carol, that you are to do what they want you to do. You don't have a choice in this. I would hate to see anything bad happen to you," Sheriff Conners said as he laughed hard and loud at my aunt.

"I guess I understand, sheriff. I don't like what you are doing. Please don't hurt my niece or her friend. They will be leaving Henderson soon and they won't cause any problems," Aunt Carol begged.

"Now, Carol, you know it's not up to me. I can't

understand why you are so worried about your niece. We can't afford for our secrets to get out. They are afraid that your niece and that fella is a threat to them. Just do as I say and you won't regret it!" the sheriff said loudly.

Jim left the area where he was standing and came back to the room where I was. He then told me not to ask any questions. He said that he had some of his own that he had to ask my aunt.

Soon after, Aunt Carol entered the room. Once more she was in a wheelchair. Jim had just seen her out on the porch, standing and walking around. There had to be a reason why she was pretending to be crippled.

"Aunt Carol, how are you today? You look well. It's nice to be here again."

"I'm fine, dear! I am surprised to see that you are still here in Henderson. I thought that you would have gone back to California by now."

"No, we won't be leaving soon."

"Mrs. Baker, I can't help but wonder why you are in the wheelchair," Jim said to her.

"Yes, Mr. Peterson, I was hurt while I was riding one of my horses. I haven't been able to walk since the accident. Why do you want to know?"

"Is that why you have so many servants helping you around here?"

"Yes, Mr. Peterson, that is why. Also, I am an old woman. I have a big place to take care of. Frankly, I find it none of your business!"

"Normally, Mrs. Baker, I would tend to agree with you. There are certain circumstances happening now that make me wonder why you would find it within yourself to lie to your own niece. I know for a fact that you can walk. When we were here the first time, I saw your legs moving. When you didn't think we could see. Today I saw you standing out on the porch, talking to the sheriff. Now I am a reporter, Mrs. Baker. It is up to me to ask questions and to get answers, even if I have to step on your toes getting them. We don't intend on leaving here until we get the answers that we came to Henderson to get. You might as well get over this act that you are putting on, and tell us what we need to know!"

"Well, Mr. Peterson! I see that you are a very brave man, talking to me like that. I tried to warn you and my niece the first time that you were here in my house. I see that neither one of you listened to me. I told you before that I wasn't going to tell you anything and I don't intend to go back on what I said now. It's true that I wanted you to believe that I couldn't walk. I have a very good reason for not telling you the truth. If I say anything, your lives and my own will be in serious danger. I would like for you to take Sarah and leave my house. I am very tired now, and I need to take a nap."

"I'm sorry, Mrs. Baker. I told you that we weren't going anywhere until we got answers, and we're not." Jim was very adamant toward my aunt. She had it coming!

I turned to her and said, "Aunt Carol, why did you lie to me? Please tell us what it is that you know. Our lives are already in danger. If you are so worried about us, you will tell us how or what we can do to stay alive. There's a story here in Henderson, and we don't have any intentions of leaving here without it."

"Sarah, I can tell you this. You are being watched. Please forget about your story and leave here today."

"Mrs. Baker, what are you so afraid of? No one is in the room except you and us. No one can hear us.

What you tell us won't be printed in the paper. Are other reporters that have come here in danger also?" Jim asked.

"If I tell you, I will be sentencing you and me to a life of hell! I guess you have every reason to know the truth about everything. Yes, the other reporters are in danger. Some of them have been found dead. The rest of the reporters that came here are missing. That is why you must take Sarah and leave, and never come back to Henderson again. I can't tell you everything here at my home. They have their ways of finding out things. There are too many people that can overhear us."

Aunt Carol looked very nervous. She got up from her wheelchair and walked over to the window to see who was outside, and if anyone was watching her house.

"Mrs. Baker, as Sarah has told you, we know that we are already in danger. We also know that the sheriff is involved in the evil that's going on around here. I don't understand how you can pretend to care about your niece and not tell her something that might save her life. How can you live with yourself? How will you feel if something bad happens to her?"

"All right, I will tell you both what you need to know. I can't tell you here. Stay away from the sheriff. He will only hurt both of you. Tonight I will meet you at your dad's old cabin. It will be after it gets dark before I can come. I have to make sure that no one follows me there."

My aunt sat back down in her wheelchair. She covered her legs with a blanket and then she took us to the front door. She acted as if we had just come by the house to have a nice talk with her. She knew that everyone that was at her house had to believe that everything was all right. It was as if she was being held prisoner in her own home.

As Jim and I walked down the path, we looked around to see who was watching us. When we reached the car, Jim looked back at the window, where he had seen Aunt Carol and Sheriff Conners talking. My aunt waved at him and we got into the car and drove away. At that moment I thought about the night that Mr. Walker was on his way to the house to talk to us. He never made it! All I could do was hope that my aunt would be safe and that nothing happened to her the way it had with him.

There was one more thing for us to do before going to the cabin. The next stop for us would be the public library in Henderson.

We drove into town and parked beside the big red brick building that had been standing in the middle of town for more than fifty years. That was the library. I was sure that there would be records of old newspapers that could help us learn more about Henderson and the old Henderson Mine.

We walked up the long stairs to the top and entered the old building. The place still looked the same.

We walked over to the woman sitting at the main desk. She was the librarian. We asked her if they had old papers there, dating back for the last ten years. She said that we could find what we needed in a large book in the back of the room.

We walked back there and, sure enough, there on a huge table was what we needed to see. We sat down and looked back ten years ago to the time when the old mine had the fire and explosion. We read about all the men that never made it out alive. Then we went over other newspapers which listed people that had mysteriously died or disappeared in town. It was true. Everything pointed to our deepest suspicion. The Nosferatu were like fiends and ghouls. The more blood and flesh they tasted, the more they wanted.

We had found out what we had come for. After closing the book, we walked away and out of the library.

We went to the car and left town. On our way to my parents' house, we saw lots of dead animals alongside the road. They were partially eaten and left there for another time of feasting. The creatures were getting restless. They were killing more and more. Some way they had to be stopped!

When we reached the old house, we could see that no one was waiting for us. Jim parked the car and we unlocked the front door. When entering, we looked everywhere. The evil ones weren't alone in wanting us dead. We had to watch every move of the sheriff and his men.

It had been a few days since Jim had spoken to Frank Cooper by phone. It was time to call before we left the house. "Frank, there's a lot going on here. Did you get the pictures that I sent you? If so, what do you think of them?" Jim asked Frank.

"Jim, I'm glad that you called me. I have been trying to get through to you and Sarah all day. There have been some new developments, and I think that you two should take the next plane back here right away. We have heard that some of the reporters from different papers have been found dead. Some have been listed as missing. I want to forget about the story on the reopening," Frank said.

"I understand why you want us to come back home right now, Frank, but Sarah and I are getting closer to the biggest story the *Ridgewood Times* newspaper will ever have! We are going to stay here for a while longer. We have been through too much in the last few days to throw it all away now. The things that are haunting the town of Henderson have become personal. We are very close to finding out information that will blow your mind. Someone could have tampered with the phone lines. I'll call you soon and tell you everything that we know." Jim hung up the phone and walked over to me.

He had talked to Frank about us not leaving Henderson. Now he felt that he should discuss it with me.

"Sarah, I know what I told Frank on the phone about staying here and seeing this thing through. I have no right to speak for you. Tell me if that is what you want to do also. Do you want to stay here and try to help the people of Henderson, or do you want to leave here and go back to L.A.?" Jim asked.

"Jim, I heard what you told Frank. If I wasn't behind you in your decision, I would have spoken up right away. I love you, and I will do whatever you want to do," I told him.

That was the first time I had actually repeated those words to him. I did love him and it was time that he heard it from me.

I then heard Jim tell me that he loved me also. He said that he didn't know how we would stop the Nosferatu, but we would find a way.

We carried some of our items to the car and locked the front door of the house. Until we knew that we were safe forever, we could never come back here.

As we started to leave, I looked back. I wondered if I would ever see the house again. Jim saw the sadness in my eyes. He put his arms around me and pulled me close to him.

"Don't worry, partner. I will take care of you. I won't let anyone hurt you. No matter what, if things get too rough, we will forget about the story and everything, and catch the next plane back to L.A., like Frank wants us to do. Now can I see that beautiful smile of yours one more time?" he said.

I gave him the best smile that I could give, and then I kissed him as he had kissed me.

We drove away. The cabin was off of the main road that went past the old Henderson Mine. It took a while to get there. Ordinarily, I would have been looking at how scenic and magnificent the scenery was, but today all I could think about was getting to the cabin without anyone seeing us.

We stopped in front and I walked closer to it. It had been several years since I had been there. The wildflowers looked so pretty. Jim walked up behind me and put his hand on my shoulder. I turned to him and smiled. It was wonderful to have him there with me.

The inside of the cabin was dusty from it being unoccupied for so many years. Jim and I cleaned it up the best way that we could. Later, we went outside to the front porch and the old swing that my dad had made for Danny and me. There was nothing more wonderful than the peace and quiet of the mountain.

When the darkness came, we went inside. All that was left for us to do was wait for Aunt Carol. After tonight, all of our questions would be answered.

At last she arrived there safely. She got out of her Jeep and walked toward the cabin. We stood there, watching, to make sure that she hadn't been followed. Now that she was here, we could find out more about the town of Henderson and the old Henderson Mine.

14

TEA AND MORE

"Aunt Carol, we are very glad to see you. I was starting to worry about you. I don't want anything to ever happen to you," I said.

"I'm sorry it took so long getting here, dear. I had to make sure that no one saw me leave the house." She took off her coat and handed it to Jim. Then she walked over to the table and sat down.

"Mrs. Baker, I'm glad to see that you kept your word and came up here. I have to tell you that I had my doubts that you would bother to show up. Now that you are here, you can tell us what the big secret is that we aren't supposed to know about." Jim hung up the coat and walked over to sit down beside her at the table.

"I can understand why you would have your doubts, Mr. Peterson. I am a woman of my word. I very seldom break my promise to anyone. You are a very brave man. Today, when you were at my house, you talked to me very firmly ... and harsh! It has been a long time since anyone has gotten away with that kind of behavior without getting thrown out of my house. I can tell that you are a kind and strong young man."

"I knew that you would help us, Aunt Carol. I know that this must be very hard on you. Please tell us what we need to know," I said.

"What I am about to tell you both will change your lives forever. Things will never be the same for you again. Are you both prepared for that?" Aunt Carol asked.

"Yes, Aunt Carol. Please go on with your story," I said.

"Several years ago, there was a young woman from a small town in Germany who had been ridiculed by the people in her town. She was very beautiful and caught the eye of every man that saw her.

"One day, the townspeople found out that she had slept with a local businessman. The man was married and had a family. The townspeople found this to be disgusting. Their law stated that if a married person was found unfaithful, they would automatically be put to death if caught. The man was shot and killed. The young woman's mother was afraid for her. She took her daughter and ran away with her into the woods. There, the girl saw an old woman that had been declared by the townspeople to be known as an old hag or a witch. The old woman made the girl lie down on a table. There she said some words over her, which changed her looks. From then on, the young woman would be ugly and undesirable to anyone who would look at her again.

"Knowing that the young woman's mother had done everything she could do to protect her daughter, she took her back into town. The townspeople took one look at her and wept amongst themselves out of pity, knowing that she would have to live out the rest of her life in shame and misery. They decided to let the young woman live, knowing that eventually she would go mad and kill herself. Days and weeks went by and the woman became very lonely and depressed. She went into a cave and starved herself to death.

"There in the cave were vampire bats. The bats lived in the forest, where they drank the blood of vertebrates. When they found the young woman's body, they drank her blood. They sank their sharp, chisel-shaped teeth into her flesh. They lapped up her blood and left her body to rot. Some of the bats didn't just drink her blood, they ate parts of her. When the bats reproduced their young, for some unknown reason their babies were born with some human features. The features they resembled were that of the young woman they had eaten.

"From that time on, the bats had the power to either be human or to turn themselves back into a bat. They were evil creatures that subsisted on the blood of the living, and they would come out of the cave at night and return to it in the morning. The creatures from then on would be known as Nosferatu. They can be destroyed with a wooden stake that is stabbed through their heart. Other ways that have been known to kill them are death by fire or water. Some of the people in the town were found dead with a hole in their necks. After a while, most of the people of the village realized what was happening in their town. So they set out to find the cave with all of the bats.

"At that time, they found the woman's body half eaten. What little bit of her that was left from the rotting was taken back to her mother for burial. The townspeople became outraged! They gathered together and laid branches and twigs in front of the cave. Then they set fire to them in hopes of burning up all of the vampire bats that were inside. Unfortunately, not all of the bats were destroyed. The remaining ones managed to escape through another opening in the cave and found their way here to America.

"Some way they came here to the town of Henderson, to make their new home in the old Henderson Mine. At that time, the mine was closed. The bats thought that they would always be safe there from the people of the town that might try to destroy them.

"As time went by, the more the bats reproduced, the meaner the bat babies became. They began coming into town at night, looking for human food again. If there was no one out and about in the night to prey upon, they would try to seduce whomever they could into letting them enter their home. A Nosferatu cannot enter a building unless they are invited. Some nights they would not eat. Eventually, they became so hungry that they would attack nearby animals that couldn't defend themselves.

"When the mine opened up again fifteen years ago, it made the creatures of the night mad, and they started getting revenge on the miners. They didn't want anyone to interfere with their way of living.

"Over the years, the people of Henderson have gotten to where they are very afraid of them. They believe that if they disobey, they too will be their next meal. The creatures have the power to change themselves into anyone that they want to be.

"They don't want you here, Sarah. They are afraid that you and Jim will try to destroy them. They can be very mean, and they will do anything they have to do."

"Mrs. Baker, Sarah and I had figured out already that there are Nosferatu in Henderson and at the mine. We were approached by a small child that was sitting in the road, eating a dead animal. Also a young woman came to me to try to entice me into joining her outside. Thank you for telling us the story of how this awful terror started!"

"I wish that I would have known about the creatures approaching you. I wouldn't have waited so long to tell you all of this. There is more to the story that you should know," Aunt Carol explained.

"Let's have some tea first. Then you can tell us more

about what you know," I said as we sat down to rest.

We drank our tea and then Aunt Carol resumed her story.

"After the mine reopened fifteen years ago, the safety inspector of the mine was making his morning check of the different sections.

"Everyone was feeling very good and happy that particular day. The company that owned the mine at that time had decided to give the workers a salary increase and a bonus to go with it.

"At that time, old Fred Parker was the safety boss. I don't know if you remember him, Sarah. Your dad and mom had him over for dinner a couple of times. Anyway, Fred was a very hard worker, but he was known for the wild stories that he liked to tell people. It had gotten so bad that no one would believe a thing that he had to say.

"That particular day, when he was checking the mine, he went into Section E. He was checking it when he ran out of there, yelling and screaming. He told Casey Smith that he had seen bats. He went on to tell how the bats were the biggest bats that he had ever seen. There was no doubt that the mine had bats. Everyone didn't question that part of the story. Other men had seen bats at one time or another. It was the way that he explained the bats that made the miners laugh at him. He told them that the bats were huge and had hair. He also said that they had pale faces, tinted red eyes, and fangs. Everyone knew that old Fred liked to take a drink now and then. They thought that it was another one of his stories.

"He even went into town with the story. No one in town would listen to him either. Everyone laughed at him. Eventually, the story died down and he forgot about it. So did the other workers. A few years later, Fred was found dead in the mine. There were different stories going around about a rock slide and how the ribs had caved in on old Fred. When they brought him out of the mine, the company tried to cover up the fact that his neck had a hole in it. It looked as if it had been half eaten. Then the story changed to where an animal must have gotten to him after he died before anyone found him.

"The people of the town accepted that and life around here went on as usual. At that time, Sarah, you were in grade school. Once again, things quieted down around the mine and in the town for a few years. No one thought too much about it. Then, one day, the company decided to dig farther into the mine, in hopes of making more money for the company.

"Once more, that was the only thing that they cared about. They were going to open up a section that never had been touched before. Your dad had been made the new safety inspector. He was sent into the new section to check things out. When he returned, he was as white as a ghost. He told the boss that there was no way the company could open up that part of the mine. He told them that it would be too dangerous. They asked him why, and he told them that he had seen something that couldn't be uncovered. He said that if he told them what it was that he had seen, it would turn their hair white! The boss of the mine didn't like your dad's answer, and he then dismissed him as the safety inspector of the mine.

"It wasn't too long after that happened when the men were forced to go into the new section. The mine suffered cave-ins, the ground shook, and rocks fell down. Some of the men got hurt and others were afraid to go back in there. With all of the accidents that were happening, the company still wanted the men to continue to mine. All the company could think about was how much money they were going to make. It seemed like the safety of the workers didn't mean much to them!

"The men continued to work, and then the day of the fire an explosion happened. I saw Bill Pratt coming from work. He was working the day shift that week. Your dad had taken the day off. Bill said that for some reason the mine had been having trouble with a small amount of methane gas that day. Some of the men had gotten sick and gone home. They had shut the mine down for a while. The fans were turned on to clear out the gas. The company thought that they had the methane problem under control. They let the men go back into the mine. The mine was expecting a train that weekend, and they wanted to meet their quota. It was shift change and some of the men were working in the new section. Others were working in other sections.

"Three workers were sent into the Section E, so that the miners that were still working in there could take their break. When they got there, they found the miners dead. They had holes in their necks and had been half eaten. This terrified the workers who had found them. They ran out of the section, yelling and screaming! This caused a major panic when the other miners heard what the men had seen in there. Some of the men grew careless with the equipment and the tools they were working with. One of the miners who had been working with a torch, in his panic, forgot and left it turned on. He laid it down and started running out of the mine.

"Before the other workers could get out, the

methane gas caused the torch to explode. The mine caught on fire. The man who left the torch on was only 19. He was a new miner who had never worked in a mine before. Some of the town wanted to string him up and not give him a fair trial. Other miners were found later on, but none were found alive.

"After the fire department got the fire out, there were people who went into the mine to try to rescue those men who were in another section that hadn't caught on fire. The men were never found. The young man who had caused the fire finally went into shock. It was more than he could handle. He was taken to a mental hospital. As for the three dead miners, they were brought out of the mine. Once again, the company blamed the accident on the explosion and the animals that were trapped inside the mine without food to eat. There was a big investigation, all right. No one would admit that whatever it was that had killed the miners may not have been human!

"When the men were removed from the mine, the company did another cover-up. They were afraid that everyone would freak out. This is about the time when they shut down the mine and the miners were left without a job. The company kept certain men employed so that they could maintain the mine, in case it sold again. The men whom they kept saw a lot of things that the company tried to keep secret. Eventually, talk spread and the people of the town found out about the creatures. Everyone became afraid of them. They had seen what they could do. No one wanted to trust anyone in the town. The Nosferatu had threatened the sheriff and the man that owned the old Henderson Mine. Because it was easy for the bats to change themselves into human form, it was hard to tell a creature of the night from that of the living!

"The miners that work in the other mines were told that if they, too, didn't cooperate with the creatures, they would also suffer. This is why everyone is so quiet and so unfriendly. I know all of what I've told you sounds far-fetched. I never would have believed it if I hadn't seen it for myself."

"You're right, Aunt Carol. All of this does sound like a tale out of a story book. If Jim and I hadn't seen the things that we've seen, we would be more shocked than we are. Why did you use a wheelchair and why are the men taking wooden boxes down into the mine?" I asked.

"Sarah, I was the one who was sending you the notes. I was trying to scare the hell out of you, so that you would leave and go back to L.A. I have a servant I can trust. The first time you got a note was when you were at the diner. I knew that you were coming to Henderson. Your mom had called me and told me that you had left. I called the airlines and got your schedule, and that's how I knew about what time you would be arriving in Henderson.

"We waited until we saw the lights on in the house, and then we saw you leave shortly after that. We followed you and Jim. When you went into the ladies' room, my servant put the note under the door. It was the same way when you came to see me the first time. The note in the mailbox was from me also. I had you followed by my servant, so that I knew where you were at all times. I had to make you believe that I was confined to a wheelchair, so that I could watch after you. I wasn't trying to fool you because I wanted to hurt you, Sarah. I love you!

"The wooden boxes are being taken into the mine

for the Nosferatu to sleep in. It probably seems strange to you that they would need to sleep whereas the mine is dark all the time. Because they were formed from a human being, that is one of the characteristics that they were given. Before they sleep, they make themselves into human form. Since the townspeople of Henderson found out about them, they have been doing things for them to help them keep their existence here. The people are too afraid not to help them."

"You have explained everything, Aunt Carol I found Dad's old journal. There was a part in it that I didn't understand until now. It had to have been when he was the safety inspector. That must have been the time when he first saw the Nosferatu. I can see why Casey and Betty Smith are so frightened to tell me anything."

"I guess we should be mad at you, Mrs. Baker, for scaring us so badly. You were only trying to protect Sarah and get us to go back to L.A. I'm sorry for being so rude to you and accusing you of not caring about your niece. I hope that you can forgive me for being so arrogant and I hope that we can be friends," Jim said as he went to my aunt and hugged her.

"I accept your apology, Jim. I truly want to be your friend. I'm sorry it took me so long to help you," she said. "Sarah, I am really sorry for hurting you in any way. As I've told you before, you must stay away from the sheriff! No good will ever come from it."

I then pulled from my jacket the snapshot of the people at the mine that I had seen the day that Jim and I first went up there. I showed it to her and asked, "Can you tell us who these people are? This was taken at the mine."

"Yes, Sarah. They are citizens of Henderson that

hang around the mine. They have been bitten by the Nosferatu, but haven't completely been transformed yet. They will do anything to help the creatures. These people are dangerous! Please stay away from them."

"Sarah, I must go back down into the mine. I need to get pictures of them for the paper. I want to do this while they are sleeping. If the Nosferatu multiply and spread all around the country, our story could help save the lives of thousands of people. I know our world isn't ready for this. I feel that we have to let them know about it any way we can. I want you to stay here with your aunt, where you will be safe," Jim said as he held me close to him.

"No, Jim! I cannot let you do this by yourself. I am going with you. It will take both of us. I am familiar with the mine. I know several places where we can be safe. Besides, I thought that we agreed that we would be partners for life." I kissed Jim and pulled myself close to him once again. Nothing would ever separate us. We would either live together or we would die together!

"Sarah, I can tell by the way that you two are acting that there is more than just friendship between you. Am I right?"

"Yes, Aunt Carol. Jim and I have grown to love each other. I have to go with him. He will need me. I hope that you understand. You are welcome to stay here, if you want to."

"I know, dear. I'm afraid that it is time for me to go back home. Please, Sarah, be careful! If they see you, they will never let you leave alive."

"We will be careful. They already know that we are in Henderson. We will try our best to stay away from the sheriff. We heard him telling some men to get rid of us. We have to go back in there. Jim is right. If those things multiply any more, they could control our universe. It would never be the same again. We must try to kill them before they kill us!"

When Aunt Carol was ready to leave, she hugged us and walked out the door. She turned to me and said, "As soon as you get what you want, leave this horrible town, Sarah. Don't look back!"

She walked to her Jeep and left. Soon she was no longer in our sight. What she had said to us was more than I could have imagined in my lifetime.

15

TRAPPED

The sun was shining over the horizon and soon it would be time for us to leave the safety of the cabin and return to the mine. After our night with Aunt Carol, listening to her tell us the story of how this mess all got started, we could see why everyone in Henderson was so afraid. If things were different and I had stayed here, I, too, would be at the mercy of the Nosferatu!

I had read many fiction books and stories about them. I never believed that they really existed. Never in my wildest dreams did I imagine that someday I would be in contact with them, and have to fight for my life against them. Everything about this town and the horrible things that were going on right now felt like it was coming from a horror film at the movies. There are many things in this world that no one can explain. This was one of them!

Jim took the wooden legs off the table and we shortened them until they were small enough to be wooden stakes. We were two grown, sensible, intelligent people trusting an old myth. It all seemed like a bad dream, and all we could hope for was that we would wake up and be back in L.A., safe and well!

After we had gotten what we needed for the mine, we left the cabin without the car and started walking through the woods until we arrived at our destination. Before we dropped down into the opening, Jim had something to say. "Sarah, it's very important that you listen to me. At all times, we must keep ourselves safe. Stay close to me and I will do whatever it takes to protect you."

We then went down into the hole. There was no turning back now!

The mine was wet, cold and dark. We turned on our flashlights and started walking. No matter how tired we both felt, we knew that we must keep going until the darkness came to us outside. At last we could hear voices up ahead. They, once again, were the voices of the sheriff and his men. We got down on the floor of the mine and turned out our lights. Then we crawled closer until we could hear what they were saying.

"I don't care what you have to say. I told you both to get rid of those nosy kids. Instead you up and lose them. I know that they are around Henderson somewhere. They are a threat to the future of the town, and this mine. You have to find them and stop them today!" Sheriff Conners said loudly. He enjoyed barking orders at his men.

"We hear you, sheriff. We almost found them at Carol Baker's house. By the time we got there, they had left. We have someone watching her house now all the time. If they go back there, they are dead."

"Right now, we have to get those boxes into the cave. Go get the truck and bring it in here right now."

"Whatever you say, boss."

"You're right. I am the boss. If you know what's good for you, you won't forget it. I'm sick and tired of you young punks thinking that you can do whatever you want to do. For many years I have done everything I could do to save the butts of everyone in this town. I'll be damned if you or anyone else is going to screw it up!" the sheriff said loudly. The men left the area. The sheriff had a violent temper, and it was apparent that his men were afraid of him.

Because the sheriff stayed behind, there was no way that we could move without being seen. We were stuck where we were. All we could do was stay and wait. It would be too dangerous if the sheriff saw us in the mine. He was out for blood ... our blood!

The longer he had to wait, the more impatient he became. He walked back and forth, waiting for his men. Needless to say, when they finally did return, he was in a worse mood than when they left.

"It's about time! What the hell took you so long getting in here? I'd been better off to have done it myself. The Nosferatu want the boxes today." He then followed his men to the rear of the big truck. There was a cave by the truck that had been formed because of the explosion that had taken place down there. Sheriff Conners watched the men carry the boxes in there, and then he walked away. When the men were done, they left in the truck. We were all alone in there with the undead from HELL!

"Sarah, we have to find a way to get out of here. Soon the Nosferatu will be walking around the mine, looking for food. Do you know of any place where we can go that might keep us safe from them?" Jim asked.

"Yes, Jim. There was a place, unless the explosion destroyed it years ago. There is an opening in the face of the mine that had been there for several years." We walked away and down the road to the hole. It was our only hope that we had to stay alive. There was a crevice in the face where Jim could put his feet in to climb into it. It was high off the floor. We knew that the creatures could smell blood. Even that place might not be enough to keep us safe!

Jim climbed up into the hole and then helped me do the same. It was going to be a long night sitting there, waiting for morning to come so that we could get out of the mine.

We hadn't been there very long when we saw a group of creatures walking around below us. They were hissing and growling with hunger. There was one that I recognized. It was Jack Winters. He was also a friend to my family. When the town looked for him after the fire, they couldn't find him. By then he was one of the Nosferatu.

We knew that we had to stop them. If we couldn't, they would keep walking around each night in the mine and the town forever.

For some reason, they didn't try to kill us. Jim and I knew that they could smell our blood. They had to know that we were up there!

All they would do is raise their ugly heads and show their blood-stained teeth. They were waiting for something. Jim and I knew what it was they were waiting for. They were waiting for us to make a mistake.

When morning came, the mine was silent once again. The evil had gone back into the caves to sleep. We got down from the hole we were in and went into the section where we had seen the sheriff and his men putting the wooden boxes. There was no time for us to waste!

When we were in the right section, we shone our flashlights all around the area. There was no one in sight.

Jim looked at me and said, "Sarah, this is where we have to split up. I'll look in the wooden boxes next to the entrance. If someone decides to come in, I can protect you. If you find anything in the boxes over there, take a picture of it. We need to work fast!"

I went across the cave from Jim and started

opening the lids. I was ready to give up when I opened one more. There, lying helpless and almost dead, was my aunt! She was tied up with a gag in her mouth. I ran over to Jim and frantically said, "Aunt Carol is in one of the boxes! I'm not sure if she is still alive."

We were unaware of the sheriff and his men behind us. He had come back into the section to see if Aunt Carol was dead or alive. When he saw us standing there, he started smiling with joy. He not only had my aunt where he wanted her, he had us too.

From out of nowhere came Sheriff Conners' voice. "I know that your aunt told you about me and the secret of the old Henderson Mine. I knew that she couldn't keep her mouth shut. When I saw her leave the house, I followed her to your cabin. I hid outside until I saw her leave. I could tell by the look on her face that she had told you everything. I decided then and there that I would keep her alive for the time being, instead of killing her. I knew that eventually I would have you kids right where I wanted you. This way, you can watch her die a little bit at a time. Then you will see what will happen to you when the creatures are finished with her. I knew that sooner or later you would be stupid enough to come back down into the mind. There's no way that I can let you leave here alive. You see, it's too bad that you nosy city kids didn't listen to me when I told you to leave Henderson!"

At that moment, Sheriff Conners' men grabbed Jim and me. We struggled to get free, but they were too strong. They tied our hands behind our backs and then tied our feet together. Aunt Carol was taken out of the box and set beside us on a rock. Then the sheriff and his men moved to the wall of the cave to watch us closely.

"Aunt Carol, are you all right? I was afraid something like this would happen to you. I knew that I shouldn't have asked you for help."

"I'm fine, dear. Don't blame yourself for this. The sheriff is a mean and evil man! Some way he would have found a way to hurt me, even if you and Jim never came here. Don't waste your time trying to save me. I want both of you to escape from here as fast as you can."

"No, Aunt Carol! We won't leave you behind. You risked your life coming to the cabin to tell us about this place. Some way we will find a way to get loose from here. Then we will all leave here together."

"Carol, don't worry," Jim said quietly. "I was a pretty good Boy Scout and I still remember about ropes and how to tie and untie different kinds of knots. Just sit still and I will keep working at this rope. Sarah is right. There is no way that we will ever leave you here to be at the mercy of those evil creatures. You were right about a lot of things. I will promise you this. I will get us out of here soon."

From the look on his face, I could see that Jim was unsure of what he had just promised us, and whatever would happen from then on. He knew that Aunt Carol was an old woman and he was trying to give her peace of mind, so that she wouldn't worry about what was to come next.

"Jim, now we know why the Nosferatu never bothered us. The sheriff must have promised them a big feast! He is really pissing me off."

Jim told me that he was glad I hadn't lost my fight to stay alive.

Sheriff Conners and his men noticed that we were talking and they came closer. As usual, the sheriff was his smug self. His eyes were glaring at me and his lip was turned up. He had a wild look in his eyes. He kept watching us.

Finally, I said, "You might think that we are a couple of city kids that can't do anything right. Well, I'll tell you this. You are in for a big surprise if you think that we are just going to let you feed us to those monsters without a fight!"

"You're wrong about one thing, young lady. I know who you are. Years ago, I worked with your dad in this here mine. I became the sheriff after you and your family left town. Your dad had a smart mouth on him, too, just like you do. It's too bad that he threatened to tell the story about what he had seen down here that day. If he hadn't done that, he might still be alive. He left me no choice. We had to do something to protect ourselves here in Henderson!"

Sheriff Conners had said the wrong thing. He stuck his face close to mine while he was talking to me. In his own words, he left me no choice. I looked into his eyes and spit in his face. Then I told him that it was true that I was my father's daughter. I also said that I had the guts to kick his sorry ass!

The sheriff could see that I was mad. I expected him to grab me and maybe kill me right there on the spot! Instead, he just laughed his crazy laugh at me, and then walked away. Now that I knew why my dad was found dead, the sheriff had made a big mistake. Before, I was so afraid that I knew no greater fear. Now I was so mad that nothing in this world could stop me from getting revenge for my father's death. If I didn't do anything else, I would make sure that Sheriff Conners never left the mine alive.

16

DARKNESS WAS NEAR

Hours passed and soon it would be dark again. We were wet and cold. Jim was still trying to free himself from the ropes that were cutting into the flesh on his hands. The sheriff was still watching us. I knew that some way I was going to distract him. I stared at him until I had his attention. He got up from the rock and came over to us.

"Is there something that you want to say to me, young lady? You act like you are awful sure of yourself. You are a pretty young thing. It seems a shame to feed you to the Nosferatu," he said as he laughed loudly at me.

"I'm not afraid of you. Everyone dies sooner or later. I have to warn you, sheriff, I won't die easily."

Once again he walked away from us. I could tell that I was pushing his buttons and I wondered how far he would let me go before he would snap.

"Sarah, please be careful what you say and do to him. He will stop at nothing to hurt you and Jim. I am an old woman who has lived her life. I don't care what he does to me, but I do care what he does to you! Don't try to get revenge for what he did to your dad."

"I know what I'm doing. Somehow Jim will find a way to get us out of here. Meanwhile, I have to find ways to keep the sheriff busy, so that Jim can work harder to free himself from the ropes. Sheriff Conners will be watching me and not him."

"No need to worry, ladies. It won't be much longer and I will be free. Then I can get us out of this horrible place."

We all knew that there was no time for mistakes now. Whatever we did in the next few minutes would mean the difference between whether or not we lived or died.

I knew that Frank must be frantic from worry. He was expecting us to call him back before now. There was no way that he could help us out of this mess that we had gotten ourselves into. The thought of getting revenge for my dad's death was the only thing that kept me going. I would find a way to get even with the sheriff.

Sheriff Conners had a smirk on his face. He stood there with his arms crossed. He knew that our time was running out and he wanted us to see him gloating about it. He looked at Aunt Carol with fiery eyes and said, "Tell me, Carol, what did you think you would gain by telling your niece everything? Didn't you know that someone would see you leaving your house? Allen Walker thought that he, too, could tell them what he knew. He should have known that it would all blow up in his face."

"I'll tell you why! I wanted her to know what kind of a person you are and what she was up against," said Aunt Carol. "I thought that she would leave this place before you could hurt her and Jim. When I left my house, I didn't think anyone saw me. All I wanted to do was protect her from you. Everyone in town knows what you and your men did to poor Allen Walker! His widow is so afraid of you that she won't tell you how much she hates you for what you did to her family. You took away her husband and nothing for her will ever be the same. I, on the other hand, am not afraid of you. You can do whatever you want with me. I will tell you this. Somehow I will find a way to stop you. I will be damned if I will let you hurt anyone in my family ever again!"

As expected, the sheriff being the cold-hearted person

that he was, laughed at her. He was crazy and felt nothing for anyone other than himself.

Darkness was here. It wouldn't be long now before the Nosferatu would be walking around, looking for food. If they found us, they would tear our bodies apart and devour us piece by piece.

At last Jim was free! What we had been waiting for finally happened. The flesh on his arms had pulled away from the bone. Blood was dripping from the wound. He sat there, pretending that he was okay and still tied up. If the sheriff didn't leave soon, there would be no way that any of us could get out of here alive.

The sheriff started laughing uncontrollably. He looked at us and said, "It will all be over with very soon. After that, you won't have a care in the world. You and your friends will be one of them. You can join them and live forever!"

"If you think that you are going to scare us with words, you are sadly mistaken. There is no way that any of us will ever be one of them! If you had any kind of decency about you, sheriff, you wouldn't be mixed up with those horrible things. Why do you destroy your own kind for them?"

"I found out a long time ago who my friends were. I was the one that the company should have asked to be the safety inspector, but instead they asked your dad. No matter how hard I tried to please the boss, I always got overlooked. When the mine shut down, I even came back in here to try to help find the men that were missing. Instead of finding any men alive, I found the Nosferatu. I was terrified of them at first. I thought that they were going to kill me and eat me, just like they had the rest of my friends that were left in here to die when the mine blew up. Instead, they asked me to help them keep their existence a secret, so that no one would try to destroy them. I made a deal with them so that they would spare my life. It's true that I have made a lot of enemies over the years. I have also made a lot of friends. You had your chance to leave Henderson, missy. You chose not to go. Now, it's time for you to pay for it!"

"Stop it! You have been complaining about not getting the job of safety inspector for years now!" Aunt Carol yelled at the sheriff. "People are tired of hearing about it. Since you insist on telling Sarah that ridiculous story, why don't you tell her how you used to come to work, smelling of alcohol? You were late getting there many times. There were days when you never bothered to call or even come in to work. That is the reason why you never got the job. I am tired of you blaming my brother for it. He would still be alive today if it weren't for you. The reason why the creatures chose you to help with their dirty work is because they could smell a rat a mile away. You are the biggest rat around here!"

What she had said made him so mad that he grabbed her and shook her. "If I was you, Carol Baker, I would be making better use of the time that you have left. You are a fine one to judge me, anyway. I can remember why your husband left you. You couldn't make your man happy and that's why you ended up a lonely old hag!"

By then the sheriff's face was a bright red with anger. My aunt had struck a nerve. She was trying to make him so mad that he would leave us alone. That was the only chance we had of getting out of the cave and the mine. He was getting very impatient again.

"They should have been here by now," he told his men. "Go look around out there and see what's keeping them. Then report back to me."

This was the opportunity that we had been waiting for.

There was no way Jim could fight Sheriff Conners and his men together. Now there was just the sheriff. The other men left and Jim waited to make sure they weren't coming back. When Sheriff Conners turned his back to us, Jim grabbed him and hit him in the back of the head with a rock. The sheriff fell to the ground. It was time to tie him up and get out of there.

"Sarah, I did it! After I untie you, untie Carol. This will give me the time that I need to take care of the sheriff before his men return. We will take him with us. He is going to be our ticket out of this place."

"Are you all right, Aunt Carol? I won't let the sheriff touch you again. I told you that Jim would find a way to help us get out of here."

"Don't get your hopes up yet, dear. We have a long way to go before we are completely safe from the Nosferatu."

We heard a noise and we looked up. We had company. Word of us being prisoners had reached town and Casey Smith. He had come into the mine to find us. He was willing to risk his life in order to help save us.

17

OUR ESCAPE

When Casey saw us, he smiled like I had never seen him smile before. He said, "I can't tell you how happy I am that I found you. I was afraid that I wouldn't make it here in time. I'm glad that I got to you before they did."

"Casey, how did you know that we were down in the mine?" I asked.

"The sheriff's men went to town bragging about how they had you held hostage down here. The news spread all over Henderson. I couldn't stand by and leave you in here. Are you okay?" Casey asked.

I was so happy to hear Casey's Irish brogue! I told him that we were fine and very glad to see him.

Jim had Sheriff Conners tied up and it was now time to get out of the mine as quickly as we could.

"Let's go! We don't have much time left. The Nosferatu are coming this way. Before I got here, I could hear them in the other section."

Sheriff Conners spouted his ugly language at me. He made it clear that we wouldn't get away, and that the creatures would get all of us before we could get out of here.

"Shut your mouth! We're in charge now! You will do what we tell you to do. You are coming with us," Jim told the sheriff.

We walked fast, in hopes of getting out of the cave and the mine before the Nosferatu could reach us. I looked behind us. Casey was right. We weren't alone.

I was sure that they thought we would be their dinner.

Sheriff Conners was dragging his feet and slowing us down. "Get going. I know that you can move faster than this," Casey said.

We had walked for quite a while when we stopped to rest. I could tell that Aunt Carol was tired. "Are you all right?" I asked her. "Are you going to be able to go on?"

"Yes, Sarah. I am tired, but fine. We have to keep going. We can't stop now. If we do, they will catch up to us."

I could see that Jim was very nervous and anxious. He wanted to hurry up and get us all out of the mine. He pulled Sheriff Conners by the arm and said, "Walk faster. You are going to do something good for once. I don't care if it kills you!"

We reached an area where rocks were starting to fall in around us. The top was weak and the air was thin. There was nothing for us to do but keep going. We walked until we entered a different section of the mine. Our worse fear came to pass. There in front of us were the people from Jackson Mountain. They were bent down on the floor of the mine. The creatures had killed the workers that were outside who were working to get the mine ready to reopen. The Nosferatu were eating them. Body parts were all over. Blood was dripping from their teeth and mouths. The workers didn't stand a chance in hell against the evil ones. We had to get out of there fast! We couldn't go in the same direction.

"What do we do now, Casey? Is there another way out of here?" I asked in fear.

Casey then took the back of Sheriff Conners' neck and shoved him in front of us for protection. "This is where the sheriff comes in handy. Right, sheriff?"

"You people are dumber than I thought you were! The Jackson Mountain people are my friends. They will never hurt me. At last I can watch them destroy all of you." Sheriff Conners sneered at us.

Was the sheriff right? Were we trapped again? We found ourselves face to face with the creatures of the night.

"We'll see who gets what, you old goat! Let's try to go back the way we came. If we make it to the other section, we stand a chance of getting out of here alive," Casey said.

As we walked away, the sheriff insisted on moving slowly again. Jim was tired of dragging him around. "There's one thing, Sheriff Conners, that I failed to tell you about myself. I was a Marine before I became a reporter. I was a damn good one at that. All the training I had taught me not to be afraid of anything. I'm not afraid of you or your dead friends! If you don't start picking up your feet and cooperating with us, I am going to make sure that you join your dead friends in hell!"

By then Sheriff Conners was moving faster and we were back in the area where the top was falling in. There was a lot of loose rock and we stumbled through the mine until we came to a place that Casey believed to be the other exit out of the mine. A big rock had fallen from the top and it was blocking the opening. It looked like we could very well be trapped in there forever!

"Help me, Jim!" Casey yelled. "Maybe we can move the rocks enough so that we can squeeze through the opening. If I'm not mistaken, there is some dynamite in a box just inside of the hole, unless it was destroyed in the fire and explosion. The only way that we will know is to work fast. I am sure that the Nosferatu are close behind us!"

Jim shoved the sheriff on the floor of the mine and tied his feet together. Then, Jim and Casey started pushing as hard as they could against the rocks.

"You will never be able to move those rocks. Soon they will be here to get all of you!" the sheriff shouted.

"Shut up, you crazy old fool! I don't want to hear anything come out of your mouth again. If I do, I'll stick my foot in it!" Jim then hit him across the face with the back of his hand.

Casey saw that Jim was going to kick the sheriff. He grabbed him and said, "Don't waste time on him. Can't you see that he is trying to make you mad? The old bastard isn't worth it. We still have the rock to move."

"I'm sorry, Casey. I know that you are right. I'll make sure that he doesn't get to me anymore."

Unfortunately, the creatures had entered the section. "Push, Jim, push! We are almost there!" Casey said loudly.

"Don't worry, Sarah, we will get out of here alive. Jim loves you and he won't let anything happen to you," Aunt Carol said reassuringly.

"I know you're right," I replied.

"The rock is moved not too soon. Go through the opening now! Sarah, you and Carol go first," Casey said.

We did exactly as Casey had told us to do. He was right. There was a box of dynamite just inside the opening of the hole. We watched him set the dynamite charge.

Jim left Sheriff Conners on the floor and helped Casey move the rock back into place. "Don't leave me in here. Come back for me! I will do anything to help you," he begged.

I could have walked away without saying anything. I knew I didn't have much time. Something told me to say what I felt, and I did. "What's wrong, sheriff? I thought that you had all of your friends to protect you. That's more than my dad had when you killed him. You made a big mistake telling me that you were the one that took him away from us. Did you actually think that I would help you get out of this place? I swore that I would get even with you. There is no way that I will ever help you." I had finally gotten the revenge that I wanted.

As Casey and Jim pulled the rock shut against the wall to protect us from the Nosferatu, we could still hear the sheriff yelling to us. "Please, don't leave me like this!" Then the yelling stopped. It was too late for him. The creatures had reached him. I stood there, watching them tear him apart, limb by limb. When they tore off his head, they ripped it from his neck. I saw blood squirting everywhere! Apparently, he didn't have as many friends as he thought.

We all walked upward until we reached the top. Casey lit the charge and told us to hurry. Then he yelled out, "Hit the ground!" We did just before we heard a huge explosion. It was so intense, it shook the hillside.

There was no way that anyone inside of the mine could have survived that. Now Sheriff Conners would burn in hell along with the rest of his dead friends. There was no way of knowing whether we had destroyed all of the creatures. Only time would be the judge. For now, Henderson was safe from harm. As for the old Henderson Mine, it would be some time before it would reopen again.

Aunt Carol put her arm around me and said, "Sarah, it's all over with. Now you and Jim can go back to L.A., where you belong. I know that nothing will ever hurt our family again."

"Yes, Aunt Carol, Jim and I are finally going back home. Nothing would please us more than to have you come with us," I said.

"I don't know if I should. My whole life has been spent here. I'm not sure if I can make it in the city."

"I'm sure that you will do fine."

"All right, Sarah, if it will make you happy. I will give it a try."

Jim, Aunt Carol, Casey and I walked down the hillside. We could see people from town gathering to watch the fire. As we drove away, the sunlight was trying to break through the clouds. We were thankful to be alive and thankful to see morning come to us once more.

18

HAPPINESS, HENDERSON, AND WHAT'S NEXT

It was early afternoon. Jim and I had just finished packing the car. Our assignment was completed. We had stayed to the end!

Because of the explosion and the fire, the mine would continue to stay closed. Unfortunately, there would still be a lot of miners without work. To our surprise, no one in town blamed us for anything that had happened. I guess that they were all relieved that the town of Henderson was theirs again.

I stood by the oak tree and gazed at the old house for one last time. The HOUSE FOR SALE sign was in place. The movers were scheduled to come and get the rest of the items. I knew that I would never come back here again. My mind was full of memories of my childhood that I had growing up here. Now it was time to leave and go back to my home in Santa Monica.

I climbed in the car with Jim and we drove to Aunt Carol's house. She was still having second thoughts about leaving Henderson. We were sure that we would have to carry her out to the car. Her entire life had been spent there. The very thought of moving to the big city scared her.

There was one last stop for us to make before we could go. We wanted to say goodbye to Casey and Betty. Both Jim and I had thanked Casey a million times for coming to our rescue down in the mine. We knew that there was no way we could have survived without him. Words could never be enough to express our feelings and gratitude. Because of his help, we could go on with our lives.

When we drove up to their house, we could see them both outside working in the yard. They saw us and came over to our car. Their faces were full of joy and happiness. They looked content and serene. I guess at that moment is when I realized that Jim and I had done the right thing the day we came to Henderson to do the story for the newspaper.

Casey told us how sorry he was for not being there for us at the beginning. He said that now he felt like he could rest because he had made it right with my dad for all the times that our family had helped his. I told him that everything Jim and I had gone through would make a great story for the newspaper. Somehow I wondered how many people would actually believe what they read. It all seemed like one horrible nightmare!

We all said our goodbyes and then we drove away. As we neared town, there were several people that were out on the street. They smiled and waved at us. That was the first time that the people in town had made an attempt to be friendly. We waved back at them and kept going. We both wanted to leave Henderson as quickly as we could.

When we reached the top of the pass, I stopped the car to look at the mountainside and the town. I happened to glance in the back seat at Aunt Carol. I saw a tear run down her face. I knew then that if we didn't go soon, she would change her mind and decide to stay behind.

Our drive back to Denver went by quickly. It wasn't long before we were back at the airport, boarding the plane for L.A.

As we flew over the mountains, I knew that a part of my heart would always belong there. Now others could feel safe and enjoy the beauty and the peace that would continue to stay there forever. I leaned back in my seat and rested against Jim. I fell asleep. Soon after I was awakened and told that we were getting ready to land.

When we entered the airport, we could see that Frank and the camera crew had come to greet us and to welcome us back home. Standing beside Frank with a big smile was Danny and the rest of the family. Jim and I were very happy to see everyone. It was great to be back in L.A. I'm sure that you guessed the best part. That's right, Jim and I are getting married!

Needless to say, everyone was consumed with joy. I don't think that it was a surprise to anyone, especially Frank. He told me later that he had known for some time that we were right for one another.

We all left the airport and went to the office for a welcome home party. I couldn't believe how wonderful it was sitting at my desk again. I was back in the world that I loved so much.

The following weeks to come were filled with fun and rest. Frank had gotten the biggest story of the decade and he was so happy that he gave us time off from work. He said that it was our reward for all the hard work that we had done. Both Jim and I agreed that Frank probably felt a little guilty for us being almost killed. In retrospect of everything, we were enjoying every minute that we had together. We spent a lot of time on the beach. Jim loves the ocean as much as I do. We both love playing and running through the sand.

The days and weeks to come were spent making plans for our wedding. We had decided that it was going to be the biggest blowout that L.A. had seen in a long time. Aunt Carol and Mom had fun helping with everything. We all wanted to make it a special day.

When our wedding day came, it was held at a church in Santa Barbara. Everyone from work and our friends and family were there to celebrate with us. Jim and I were standing in front of the minister, repeating our vows. Soon it was over with and we were married. We were excited about our new life together.

From the church we went to our reception. The time that we spent there was great, but it was time for us to leave. I tossed the bouquet and we climbed into the limousine that Frank had waiting for us. I turned my head to look at our guests and that is when I saw something I was not prepared to see!

I saw Jack Winters standing by a tree. At least I thought I did. I rubbed my eyes and looked again. He was still there. Suddenly, in my mind, I could hear what Jack was telling me. I had never experienced anything like that before. I could actually hear, and understand, what he was saying. He said that their leader had not been destroyed. What was left of them was leaving Henderson and going to another place to gain strength and safety. He reassured me that Sheriff Conners was dead and that he would not be able to hurt our family. There would be a time in the future that we would need to be aware of. He said that someday the leader might try to get even with us.

I watched Jack vanish from my sight. This time I knew that it was real! Because of this, it led me to ask several questions. How long would it be before the leader of the Nosferatu came here to seek revenge? Were the problems with the creatures over with, or were they just beginning? Most of all, was this going to be the beginning of a wonderful and exciting life together for Jim and me, or were we headed for a short life that would end with us being back in hell?

Unfortunately, there was no way of knowing for sure what would happen in our future. Only time would tell what was waiting for us.

I spoke the words, "THE END!"

I looked at Maggie's face and again she had a smile. She loved the journal and the true story inside of it.

When I looked around at the passengers who had been listening to the story, a bunch of them looked like they had seen a ghost. I got asked many questions, like "Who are you? How were these people related to you? Did the Nosferatu return to kill Jim and Sarah?" Also, one person said that the story sounded like something that had been made up and that he hadn't heard of any such creatures. Apparently, this man was in denial, and I just told him that the story was real, but for him to believe what he wanted to.

I also answered all of the other questions that were asked of me. The flight attendant said that was the best story that she had ever heard and that she was cheering when Sarah, Jim, Carol and Casey not only got even with the Nosferatu, but also the no-good sheriff! I smiled at her and told her that was always one of my favorite parts of the story, and that Sarah and Jim were my parents.

I also told them a brief summary of what Clark and I had gone through in Limerick to save the town. Once again, I didn't know if anyone believed me, but Maggie did. She had heard the stories many times. In spite of the doubters, the others that had listened said that story was better than any movie they could have watched on the plane. I assured them again that it wasn't just a story made up, and that it was a true story.

It wasn't long after I had spoken when the pilot announced that we were getting ready to land in Denver, Colorado. This would be the first time for both of us to visit Henderson. I didn't know what to expect when we got there and only hoped for the best.

With several hours of driving up the mountain to the town, we had arrived. The town was very old and the people walking around looked content. Nobody waved at us, but that was to be expected. We were strangers to them.

Our first stop was to go to Pete's Diner, like Mother and Father had gone to. If it was still standing, it had to be pretty rundown by now. As we approached it, I saw that it was still open. I parked the car and Maggie and I walked into it. The people didn't stare at us like the people did to Mother and Father, so maybe this was a good sign that everything was still all right in the town of Henderson.

Shortly after we sat down at a table, the waitress came to ask us what we would like to order. She sounded pleasant enough, so Maggie and I told her what we would like to eat and drink. When we were finished and had walked to the cash register to pay, I asked the cashier if the people in Henderson were still happy, and if the old Henderson Mine had finally reopened after all the years it had been shut down from the explosion.

The cashier was very young and the only thing she said was that she guessed that everyone in town was happy and that the old Henderson Mine was still closed and probably would never open back up again. I thanked her for her input, and Maggie and I left.

From there we went to a motel in town and discussed our plans for tomorrow. The motel clerk was friendly enough and it appeared that the town was secure, like it was after Mother and Father helped Casey blow up the mine and kill the Nosferatu. I guess time would tell.

The next morning Maggie and I showered, dressed and left our room. We were on our way to look at the old house that Mother had lived in, and also the cabin that belonged to my grandfather and grandmother. The sky was blue and we had a nice day to explore the town and area of Henderson.

Many years ago, Mother and Father had given me directions on where the house and cabin were located. I took the same highway that they had driven on. For me, it was like going back in time and living the life that they were having at that time. A part of me wondered if they would have made a trip back here to look around if they were still alive.

When we reached the old house, I could see some kids playing in the yard and their mother was hanging up clothes on the old clothesline. We sat there for a while and watched. I wanted to ask the lady if we could go inside and look around, but if I did, there would be too many questions for me to answer, and I didn't want to explain to the lady why we had come back here after decades of not owning the house ourselves.

Our next stop was the old cabin. As far as I knew, it still belonged to the family. I had asked my brother, Mark, about it and he told me that when both Mother and Father had passed away, there was nothing in the will stating that the cabin had been sold. He thought that it still belonged to the family. Knowing this, when we got there, I was pretty confident that it would be safe to go inside and look around.

The drive up the mountain to the cabin was beautiful. The wildflowers were blooming all over the place, and the air smelled clean and not sour. When we finally reached the cabin, I parked the car and we walked up the small trail leading to it. The door was unlocked, so I opened it to look around, asking as I did if anyone was inside it.

No one answered me back, so we went in. I could see that it was dusty and dirty from many years of no one going there. There were lanterns sitting on the table that I was picturing in my mind that Mother and Father had used the night that they had met Aunt Carol there, and heard the story about the Nosferatu. Also, I found a small shirt that I was sure belonged to my mother that she had left behind that night.

Just looking around the cabin gave me a certain kind of peace that I hadn't felt for a while. Maggie, of course, was all excited as she looked around at all the old pictures on the walls, and other things that were old and outdated. Before we left, Maggie said that she was going to take the pictures and other things with her as she might not make it back there again. I told her that would be a good idea.

After a couple of hours in the cabin, we decided that it was time to leave. I wanted to drive past Casey and Betty's old home, to see if they were still alive. I also had directions to get there.

Their old home was still standing and Betty was still alive. From pictures that Mom had showed me of Betty many years ago, I could see that she had aged a bunch. I stopped the car in front of her home. Betty was sitting in an old rocking chair out on her porch. She had a hand-held fan and was fanning herself and watching us walk up toward her.

"Is your name Betty?" I asked.

"Yes, that is my name. Who are you, and why do you ask?" she replied.

"My name is Amy Peterson Allen. This is my granddaughter, Maggie. We originate from Limerick, Ireland. I was born and raised in L.A. My parents are Sarah and Jim Peterson. I am sure you remember them."

"Oh yes! I could never forget them. How are they? My husband, Casey, was from Ireland. He passed away a few years ago. He was a hard worker, and one day he was out on his tractor and keeled over from a heart attack. It sure has been lonely here without him," Betty commented.

"I am sure it has been. Mother and Father always spoke highly of both of you. They told me that your husband saved their lives in the old Henderson Mine. I know you are very proud of him. My father passed away about ten years ago, and my mother went to her reward around four years ago. They ended up buying the *Ridgewood Times* newspaper, and my brother Mark was put in charge of it. He, to this day, continues to run it. Has the old Henderson Mine reopened since the explosion?"

"No. After that the company that bought it decided that it would be better to keep it boarded up and closed. News was big back then, and there wasn't a miner around that would work for them if they reopened it -- out of fear. Life has been calm around here since then. What brings you and your granddaughter to Henderson?" Betty asked.

"While growing up, I told her many stories about what took place when Mother and Father were here.

Mother kept a journal and she wrote in it, telling every occurrence from the time before she and Father left L.A. until after their wedding. Maggie wanted to come back and see where some of her roots originated, and so I gave her this trip as a gift when she graduated from law school. I hadn't been here either, so it was also a trip for me as well. Has there been any word of any more Nosferatu in the area, Betty?" I asked.

"No. Not that I know of. I hardly make it into town as you can see, I am very old. I have someone bring me food from time to time. I hardly get any visitors being out this far from town. I am happy that you and Maggie stopped by to visit me," Betty said.

"We are too, Betty. It is a pleasure to meet you and visit with you," I replied.

Maggie and I stayed with Betty for a couple more hours. I told her about the gift I had inherited from my mother and my grandmother, and told her that Maggie also had the gift of what I referred to as Mind Power. I also told her about what Clark and I had endured in Ireland, and that we had fallen in love, just like my mother and father had. She was not surprised to hear that the Nosferatu had traveled to a different place besides Henderson, to make their home. She said she wondered if they had gone to other places as well.

I told her that I had wondered the same thing throughout the years. Finally, it was getting late in the day and Maggie and I were telling Betty that if we could, we would stop in again to visit with her before we left town. Betty said that she looked forward to our next visit.

On our way back to town, Maggie and I agreed that it was nice putting a face to a name and an old picture of Betty and Mother. As far as we knew, the Nosferatu were all either dead in and around Henderson, or they had managed to get out some way like the leader did, and had made their home elsewhere.

The next day, Maggie and I had planned to rent some horses and travel like Mother and Father did to the old mine. We were more or less doing what they had done when they had been here. It was a blast from their past.

That morning we went to a place not far from the old homestead and rented some horses for the day. I was amazed at how well Maggie rode as she had inherited her great-grandfather's talent of being able to do tricks on the horse. I, on the other hand, just knew how to ride and keep from falling off of one.

We kept riding until we had reached the old mine. It was nothing like Mother had explained it to me as being. We could see that it was still boarded up and pretty much leveled from the explosion. The grass around it had grown and the wildflowers that were there many years ago had started growing back. There was no odor or sour smell indicating death. We saw no one standing on Jackson Mountain, and that was a good indication that everything was calm there and that the Nosferatu had either died there or had moved on just to Ireland or to someplace else. We even rode our horses close to the mine.

Our trip back here was worth it. It gave us a chance to relive history that my mother and father had created many years ago. We had met Betty and had eaten at the same diner that Mother and Father had eaten at. We saw the old homestead and the cabin that is owned by the family, and we saw for ourselves that Henderson and the old Henderson Mine were free of danger now. Our time was about up and it would mean another long trip back to Ireland tomorrow.

When we rode past Betty's house again, we stopped briefly to tell her goodbye. She was very happy to talk to us again as we were her.

We returned the horses to the rightful owners and thanked them for letting us rent them and relive a part of my mother and father's past. It was time to go back to the motel and wait for morning to come.

That night Maggie and I had a hard time sleeping. We both had a visit from Mother. She was very adamant about relaying a message to not just me, but to Maggie as well.

We both sat up in bed at the same time, and in front of us we saw Mother standing before us. Maggie looked at me as I did her.

"Grandmother, this has never happened to me before. Please tell me what to do," Maggie said.

"Listen with your mind, child. Your grandmother has something that she needs to tell us that is important," I responded.

I told Mother that it was good to see her again and that I was going to communicate with her through my mind. Maggie told her the same thing.

"Amy, I am happy that you and Maggie came back here to Henderson, and to relieve something that your father and I did many years ago. I wanted you to see for yourselves the beauty of the area now and the town of Henderson. The old Henderson Mine is calm now. Betty is right. When your father, Casey and I blew up the mine, they traveled to Ireland. You were able to destroy the leader that was here in Henderson. That is why Limerick has stayed calm and peaceful all these years.

"There is one more leader of the Nosferatu left that

now is back in Germany. As far as I know, our family is no longer a threat to them, but there might come a time when Maggie will need to go to them and stop them as I did, and you have. I don't want both of you to worry. If I need to, I will appear before you again. I love you both!"

Mother had vanished like Grandmother had, and I knew that my suspicions were right. The ones that didn't die in this mine and in the one in Ireland had returned to Germany, where they originated from. Maggie was aware of what she might need to do, and it was the same for me. This was the first time that Maggie had a visit, and she used her mind to listen to the words that Mother spoke. We were both happy to see her once again.

The next day we left Henderson and drove to the Denver airport to take our long flight back to Ireland. That was our home and always would be.

As the plane left the ground, Maggie looked at me, thanking me for the gift that she had not only inherited from me, but the gift that I gave her of reliving her great-grandmother and great-grandfather's time that they had spent in Henderson.

I explained to her that I wasn't sure how much time I had left on Earth, but if she got called upon after I was gone, I, too, would come and be with her if she needed me to be. With Mother's words, it sounded as if our family for many generations would be destined to fight the horrible creatures. The Nosferatu, commonly known as vampires, were going to live on for many years, and all we could do was try to stop them.

Other Books by Jana Nolan

THE OLD HENDERSON MINE
(original)

MIND POWER

SOUNDS OF FEAR

SECRETS OF SLEEPING INDIAN MOUNTAIN

PURE VENGEANCE

THE UNEXPLAINABLE

DEPRIVATION

Visit her Author Web site at
JanaNolan.com